CADY HAMMER

The Ivy Labyrinth: Volume 1

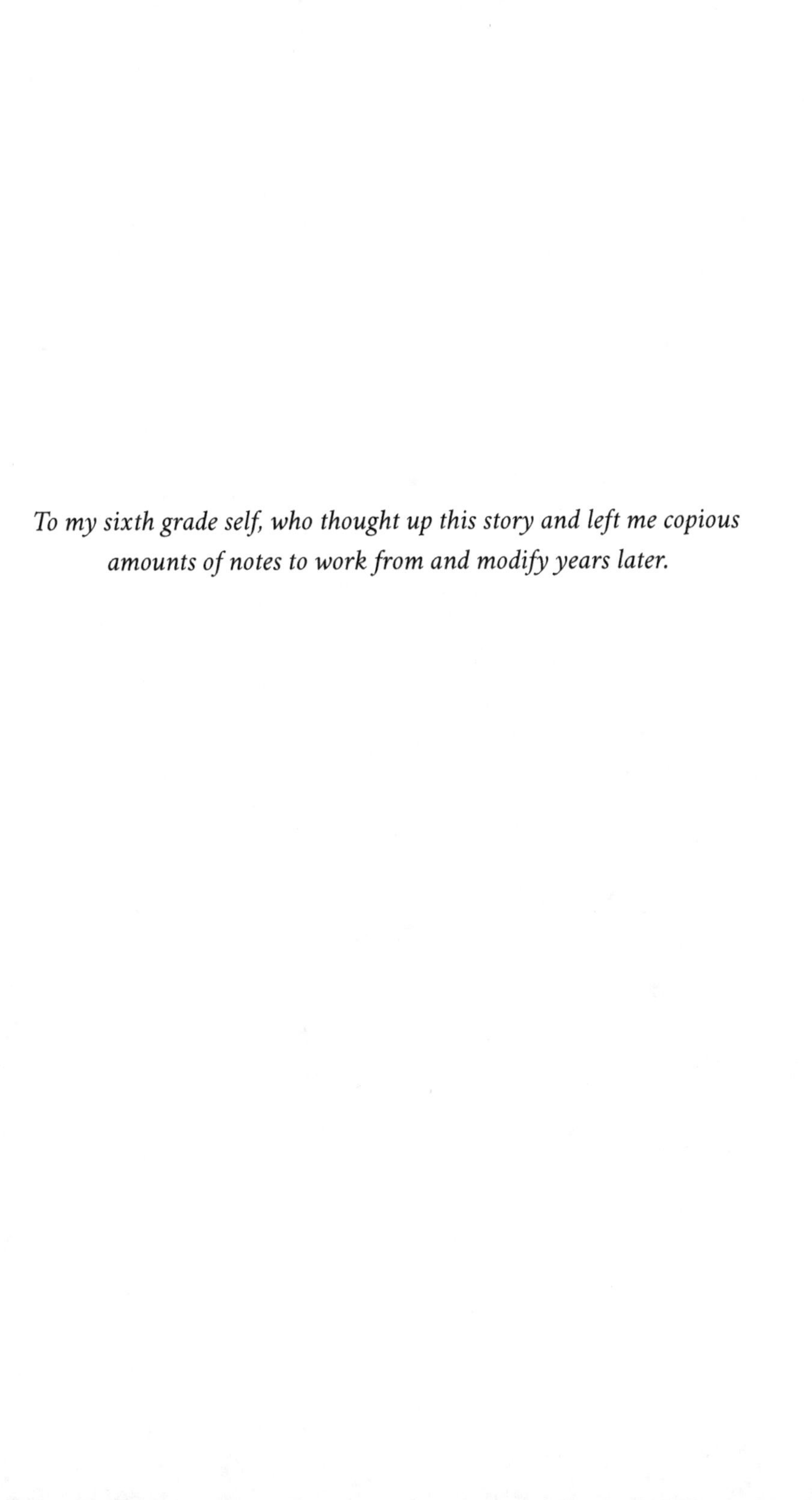

To my sixth grade self, who thought up this story and left me copious amounts of notes to work from and modify years later.

Contents

1

Kristy - Our Moment Has Arrived

Have you ever felt like there was a barrier between you and the best version of yourself? Like you couldn't quite figure out how to get from where you were now to the person you wanted to be? I feel like that every day.

I'm not the loudest person in the world. But I have a lot to say if anybody had the time to listen. My parents are always off at work, and school isn't much better because I can't raise my head up long enough from the floor to hold a proper conversation with classmates at school. And even if I could hold a conversation, I'm sort of at the bottom of the interesting creature chain. I have no magic. Yep. Just a mortal. Seventy-five percent of the students at my school, Charlotte Unitatis Magicae Academy, have some sort of power or mystical heritage, and I'm just... here.

All around the city of Charlotte, I can't go more than a block before running into someone with fascinating powers that makes me feel small. You can find all kinds of incredible beings in the area: dragon shapeshifters and elemental Fae, naiads, vampires, satyrs, elves. They all occupy their own little neighborhoods and come together downtown to run stores and restaurants and everything. And in everything they do, they bring just a hint of magic. I love watching them whether it's a dragon shapeshifter creating fire-roasted mastery on the grill or a werewolf cutting hair with a focused speed and dexterity that I wish I had. I wish I had any of it, really. It's hard to live in a world where you're always seen as second best. Even last best.

The only thing I have going for me is my brain. My brain is unmatched. I'm not saying that to brag or anything; people have been telling me that my whole life. I got the reputation of being the nerd girl early in life. I don't really mind though. I have always been fascinated by the unknown. I go chasing it, actually. I love to study the history of ancient places and ancient societies, and I'm an avid student of hieroglyphic languages. I may not speak up much, but in the classroom, my head is buried deep within my books trying to absorb everything I can. I'm a decent writer, but terrible at verbal communication. It's a wonder I manage to have friends at all with my social anxiety.

But all of that might change soon.

Today is the day that all high school students live in fear of: the day the Grand Council announces which school that the Ivy Labyrinth team will be pulled from. Essentially, the planet has been in turmoil for centuries. Every year, we are wracked by intense superstorms, earthquakes where there are no fault lines, and spontaneous explosions of land and sea. Outside of that, magical creatures are finding their magic triggered and tempered by unexplained magical phenomena. All of that unstable energy is centered in one place, a tiny island in the middle of the Atlantic Ocean containing an impenetrable labyrinth with high ivy walls. No one knows for sure how large it is or what lies inside of it, but every year, they send a group of students into it to try to break its curse.

Every year, four students are diverted from their chosen path, pulled from school, and thrust onto the island in hopes to restore magical balance to the planet. Not exactly a small feat, let alone something that high school students could achieve. But here the government goes, sending teenagers into the maze year after year. Rumor has it that it is one from our city this year. Each of the schools in the area usually holds an assembly where the high school students watch the international announcement being made. Which I'm currently very, very late for.

I rush down the wide stone steps, barely landing on every step as I head towards the large brass auditorium doors. Flinging the left one open with one hand, I slip inside and dart towards the stage doors. I catch a couple disapproving looks from administration members I don't recognize, but luckily, my favorite history professor, Professor Darkling is ushering the last stray students inside. "Just in time, Kristy," he nods at me as he waves me through. I flash him a grateful smile before turning the corner.

The theater is packed. The big screen pulled down over the black curtains is already running the news story on mute as the last few people find seats. There's a mix of creatures all over the room: nymphs flirting with satyrs, goblins roughhousing with werewolves, and the sirens gossiping in the back corner of the theater. Scanning the crowd, I spot my best friend, Brianna's signature curly hair sticking up over one of the seats down somewhere in the middle. To my relief, she's saved me an empty seat on the aisle. Trying to keep my head down to hide my embarrassment at being late, I crouch and slightly jog to take a seat.

"Thanks girl," I whisper to Brianna. "Traffic was a mess this morning."

"Uhuh," she raises an eyebrow at me. "How many times?"

I blush at the accusation. "Three."

"Three snooze buttons? Kris, you can't sleep in on a day like today! Are you kidding me?"

"I'm sorry! I stayed up too late last night reading; I only had like ten chapters left."

"And how many pages was that?"

"… 100 or so."

"Knew it."

I stick out my tongue at her, forgetting where I am for a minute. Whenever I'm with Brianna, everything in me relaxes. I loosen up and have a little more fun when I'm around her. We've been friends since middle school, and she's my ride or die in every way. She's the complete opposite of me; bold, confident, and personable, and I love her for it. Too bad we don't have any classes together this year.

"Shh." I motion for her to be quiet as the tech director finally unmutes the live broadcast. The full Grand Council, our governing body, sits at a semi-circular table at the international headquarters in Switzerland with one member from each class, magical and mortal. They wait patiently as a herald steps up to the microphone. "And now introducing the Grand Council Chief, Vampire Representative Dr. Elliot Hemlock." A tall man in a smart, high collared suit moves over to the announcer and shakes his hand before stepping up to the podium. The auditorium quickly hushes. Brianna reaches over and grips my hand tightly. I notice several other friends and relationship pairings doing the same thing. We're all nervous. Perhaps a few are a bit excited like me, but most of us are just nervous.

Dr. Elliot begins to speak. "Citizens, we have come to yet another spring where we must face our yearly challenge of navigating the Ivy Labyrinth once more. Every day, we are faced with extreme magical instability from the Atlantic region that regularly impacts our global community. Every species, magical and mortal, has been affected whether by the magical implications or the aftereffects including larger-than-average storms and massive earthquakes that decimate parts of the globe. Over 250 years ago, after scouting the area of origin further, my predecessors discovered a large intricate labyrinth sitting on an island that had practically risen from the ocean with a simple message carved into the dirt: solve the puzzle, or civilization will fail."

Murmurs make their way around the room. As elementary and middle school students, we are taught this history and its implications for us as young people. This isn't new information to us. Yet every freshman who arrives at high school still trembles in awe of its story when the announcement arrives every year. The implications on our lives for the four years we remain here, five if we fall behind, could be life-altering. Or life-ending.

"The Grand Council of the time knew it had to take action, unsure of the timeline of which they had to save their budding world," the Chief continues. "It began sending people one at a time into the maze. No one ever came out. They sent communications in, messengers and magical means. They never received anything back, and those they sent in also did not return. A few decades later, they were sending dozens and dozens of people of varying ages and technical skill inside every month or so until the Labyrinth brought hell down upon the earth. The Year of Darkness."

I remember learning about the Year of Darkness last year in my junior history class. Almost 150 years ago, the ground suddenly wouldn't produce as many crops as before no matter how much magic was poured into it. Lakes and rivers dried up, the ocean started to flood coastal cities and towns, and everything all over the world rapidly began to crumble to natural disasters. Many people perished. It wasn't as bad as it could have been, but the Labyrinth had sent a clear message. However many the Grand Council was sending inside was too many.

I tune out the Chief as he continues on with the history of the event. The reigning Chief always gives pretty much the same speech, almost word for word. He goes through how it took decades of research and experimentation for the world's top mages and scientists to realize that the best course of action was to send four and no more than four young adults into the maze. The administration wanted to make the process as fair as possible while also still making sure people were qualified in whatever way they wanted, so the Grand Council began to select one school a year from which four high school students shall be chosen. Applications have always been mandatory, and heavy fines and occasionally jail time are given to the families of students who refuse to comply. The whole practice is authoritarian in nature. I've never been comfortable with it. But eventually, this maze may kill us all. It's a moral dilemma for sure.

"Now for the selection." I hear Dr. Elliot finish his speech, and I am forced to concentrate again. The man on the screen takes a slow breath. Every year, it looks like it pains him to read the name on his little notecard. I imagine these decisions are not made lightly.

The Chief motions for an attendant to hand him the sealed envelope with the results. Brianna tightens her grip on my hand, and I follow suit. The man slowly opens the envelope and takes out the card. I can sort of see the imprint of curly handwriting in pen on the other side. "The chosen school for this Labyrinth cycle is... Charlotte Unitatis Magicae Academy."

My heart stops in my chest as the auditorium dissolves into chaos with a mixture of reactions all over the room. Some people are cheering. For them, the Labyrinth is a chance to prove themselves to the world or escape a tumultuous family life. Others are crying. To them, if they were chosen it would screw up absolutely everything in their lives. They are scared to leave their families. Many of the teachers around us are staring off into space, wondering which of their students they will lose next.

There is glory in being a Labyrinth adventurer... but no one has ever come back before. Anyone who enters wants to be the first, but the chances are low.

I don't know how I feel. A lot of me is afraid. There are plenty of chances that it could be me going, and who knows what awaits on the inside for me. But it could be the opportunity of a lifetime to solve the greatest puzzle of all time.

I look over at Brianna. Her expression is guarded as she studies mine. She makes a little motion to me, and I know to meet her as soon as we step outside. The principal makes a brief speech about how every student needs to stop by the office sometime today to pick up an application form before dismissing us back to our abridged class schedule. My best friend and I dart to the side door and escape the crowd to one of the piano practice rooms.

As soon as I shut the door behind us, Brianna squeals loudly in panic and launches into a mini rant. "Can you believe this? What if one of us ends up being picked? What if both of us do? What about my family? What about college? Nobody ever comes out of the Labyrinth!" She gasps. "We could die!"

I grip her shoulders and shake her lightly. "Brianna. Breathe." She takes a shaky deep breath. "We will get through this. The chances of us getting picked are slim. And even if we were picked, you and I are both smart enough to fight like hell to stay alive. Got it?" She exhales and grips my shoulders in return. We stand in solidarity, staring at each other for a while and grounding ourselves. I let go first. "Let's head to class. I'll meet you at lunch, we'll go to the office together and pick up our paperwork. Okay?"

"Deal," she says. We bump fists before exiting the practice room.

Here's to whatever's coming next.

2

Kai - What We Do To Get By

There is nothing better than feeling that adrenaline of being a goal down with less than ten minutes left in the game. It really gets my blood pumping.

I tear down the field after the opposing player headed my way, intent on stealing the soccer ball right out from under him. His feet dribble the ball back and forth as he searches for an opening with a teammate. I don't give him the chance though. He's left me a space. With a quick kick, I snake the ball between his legs and sprint down after it. My teammates and I drive towards the goal. My best friend, Ash, flashes me our hand signal for 'open', and I fire the ball over to him. He dodges a defender and sends a powerful kick, delivering the ball to the goal. We pass each other a quick low five before getting back to business.

This is how we do it every week. We run scrimmages every day after school until dinner, and every Friday, we kick the shit out of every school in the surrounding area in regular-season games. I'm serious, we have the best team in the division. Charlotte Pagan Conservatory is the only one coming close to beating us this year. The juniors this year are going to have to keep an eye out for them next season if they want to keep our winning streak going. But until then, we will just show them how it's done.

Conri Jenkins on our sideswipes a ball from another offensive member, and we're headed back down the field. We move in seemingly erratic, yet carefully planned patterns down the field, never straying from our positions. Michael punts the ball down to me, and I lay a nice easy boot into the corner of the goal. The goalie dives and just misses it as it hits the back of the net. The crowd goes wild, and the boys and I bask in the glory of it all.

What a way to end such a chaotic day.

When the team heads in to hit the showers, the Ivy Labyrinth is all I can think about. As soon as the announcement came up this morning, my parents gave me a call to make sure I swung by the office and picked up my application. They're always calling on me to do this stuff like I can't handle it without their help. They were excited, more excited than I have seen them in a while. Of course, there's the whole 'might never come back' thing, but it's the glory that attracts them. Another move in the playbook for them as parents with a social ladder to climb.

I don't know how I feel about it, honestly. It's more likely than not I won't be chosen. There are a thousand kids in this school for them to choose from. Statistically, I'm in the clear from certain death. In a couple months, I'll have graduated, gone off to my parents' alma mater, and be playing soccer on a scholarship or something. My parents will be attending every home game and arranging for me to meet all kinds of alumni and business contacts, etcetera, etcetera. And I'll be back on my daily grind: studying, smiling, playing soccer, and shaking hands. Nothing changes for me.

But if I'm honest, part of me thinks about a different kind of life. One with danger and adventure around every corner. Where you don't know where you're going to sleep every night. Where there's something… more to the day. A purpose. I don't know; if I ever tried to express these thoughts out loud, something tells me they wouldn't come out right.

After toweling off and getting dressed, I'm looking for Ash as I exit the locker room. He usually waits around for me so we can figure out what our plans are for the night. More often than not, he's back at my house for as long as he possibly can before heading back home. He's not doing so well with his parents.

And sure enough, as I turn the corner, there they all are having another hushed argument with lots of harsh glares and strangling hand motions. I'm not surprised. I feel bad for him. Can't be easy being the son of the governor when everyone has expectations of you that you don't meet. As always, I jog over to interrupt.

"Mr. Jackson," I interject, thrusting out my hand to the governor with a winning smile. "How nice to see you again, sir."

"Kai, my boy," he responds, shaking my hand. The man's whole demeanor completely changes from disappointed businessman to magnanimous politician. "What a game out there today."

"Thank you, sir. Glad you enjoyed the game."

"And that winning goal! The team is lucky to have you. They're going to miss you when you head to college next year."

"Team's lucky to have both of us seniors showing the freshmen how it's done."

"Yes," Ash's father says, restrained while patting his son on the shoulder. Ash flinches. "Good on both of you." When he withdraws his hand, my friend visibly shifts his body weight away from his father. His mother glares at him in that piercing way that makes me tense up. "Will I see you at home tonight, Ash?"

"I'll be at Kai's for dinner, and we've got work to do on a project," he answers quickly with a glance over to me.

"Yeah, we got work to do tonight," I cover for him.

"Alright then, well you two had better get a move on. I'll see you at home, Ash. Remember what we discussed." With that, he takes his wife by the arm, and the two of them start on towards the parking lot.

Ash turns to me. "Thanks, man."

"Anytime, man. Meet me in the guest house, alright?"

"Yep."

We head separate ways to our cars and make our way back to my house.

* * *

When we arrive at the gated neighborhood, I give a wave to the security camera before pulling into the quiet street. After a few turns, I pull up into one side of the large driveway. Ash whips in beside me, nearly taking out my right side mirror. Rolling my eyes, I get out and slam the door shut. "Man, you have got to stop doing that!"

"Chill, Kai. I haven't taken out your mirror yet, and I don't plan on it."

"At least don't cut it so close." Ash laughs and messes with my hair. I knock his arm off me and slap the back of his head. Bypassing the front door, we head around to the guest house which has basically been our designated hang-out spot since we were kids. We've practically moved in full-time with how much Ash sleeps over.

My friend throws himself onto the couch while I grab us two sodas out of the fridge. "Come on," he groans. "Can't we drink something stronger after the day we've had?" Ash enjoys a good drink every now and again, as do I, but the two of us had agreed to keep drinking to Fridays and Saturdays. Ash doesn't need to be an alcoholic on top of everything else, and I kinda feel responsible for him.

"You know the rules." I throw a can over his way, and he catches it with one hand.

As I pull my bag out and finger through the application forms for the Ivy Labyrinth team, Ash begins to play around idly with a fireball he's generated. I barely look up and scold, "Hey man, stop doing that. You'll light the couch on fire. Again."

He extinguishes the flame. "Dude. You're a dragon shapeshifter. You gotta be more chill around fire."

"When you learn to control your elemental powers, maybe I will."

"Dragon boy."

"Fae bitch."

He rolls his eyes and sits up on the couch. "What are you looking at?"

"The application for the Labyrinth stuff. It's weird. There's a lot of questions in here, not just about skill sets, but also about compatibility with others. Who we might want to go with, that kind of stuff."

"Makes sense to me," Ash shrugs. "They probably want to make sure whoever they send in doesn't kill each other in there. It's gotta be intense. Emotions running high. Maybe they're planning on putting friend groups together so they know they'll get along. Who knows what those deciders are thinking."

"Think you and I will land the gig?"

To my surprise, my friend scoffs. "I won't be applying."

"What?" I'm shocked that he's willing to risk the penalties of not applying.

"That's what my parents wanted to talk to me about after the game. They don't want me applying. They're willing to pay the fines, and they already found somebody in the administration ready to cover their tracks so it doesn't go public."

"Wow, man." I lean back in my chair. "That's wild. Why?"

"Trying to keep me under their noses, that's why. Need to control every damned aspect of my life to make sure I don't ruin their image even more." Ash may sound sarcastic here, but I can tell he's putting on a front.

"What's your plan then?"

"What am I supposed to do? I'm never going to escape from under them. They'll know I submitted paperwork if I try."

"Do you want to apply?"

"Hell yeah, I want to apply. I'd gladly go to the ends of the earth to escape these people."

"Then why don't you fill out a packet?" I slip him over the extra I had picked up in case he forgot. "I'll turn ours both in myself. We can do it tonight, and your parents never have to find out."

"Unless I'm picked."

"Unless you're picked…"

We look at each other for a second. His facial expressions change rapidly in the span of only a few seconds before he snatches the forms from my hands and picks up a pen. "Name: Ash Damien Jackson," he says grandly as he writes.

I laugh. "You are not reading the whole damn form out loud."

"Watch me."

3

Brianna - The Worst Day of My Life

When the four students were chosen to take their stab at the Ivy Labyrinth, I never thought I would be one of them.

And I never thought things would unfold so fast.

The day when the announcement came of who was chosen was anything but normal. The admin decided to arrange the assembly for midday after lunch because they wanted the students to at least attempt to learn that day. But no one paid attention. Why would we? Four fates were going to be changed literally forever in only a few hours, and they wanted us to focus on algebra? No way. Ridiculous.

For me, I couldn't concentrate for shit. It had only been a week since the school was chosen, and I'm not sure I absorbed anything from any of my classes. Thank God Kristy got me the notes from some of her class sessions. How that girl manages to work and study through mental crises, I have no idea. But I'm grateful for it. As much as she plays this very shy, quiet role at school, she's honestly a powerhouse once you get to know her. She's my rock.

But anyway, back to the announcements. The school funneled us into the poorly lit auditorium again to sit and wait in nervous silence. The governor, Robert Jackson, stood waiting at the podium to speak.

He has a son in my grade, Ash. I feel so bad for that father. Ash is an asshole, plain and simple. He's always getting into some kind of trouble, and someone is always bailing him out or giving him another chance. He's one of the athletes and a Fae, and he wanders through these halls like he owns them. I can't stand it. Everything in the world has been handed to him, and he's just wasted it.

When everyone had filed in, Governor Jackson stepped up to the microphone. "I'm not going to mince words," he said. "This is a stressful enough morning for all of us. The state wishes the students well as they embark on this journey, and we as a community will pray for their safe return." He shuffled a small group of papers before pulling out a thicker piece of stationary. When I squinted, I could sort of make out the letterhead of the Grand Council. "The students chosen to enter the Ivy Labyrinth this year are..."

"Kristy Fitzpatrick." I let out a gasp, and those around me turned to stare at us. Kristy's eyes looked like her soul left her body as she sank back into her chair next to mine. She gripped the arms of the seat until her knuckles turned white. I was terrified for her. My best friend was going to leave me. My mortal best friend was going to leave me and head off to her doom on an abandoned island in the middle of the ocean. What am I going to do without her?

"Kai Anderson." The senior dragon shapeshifter's name was read, and the attention immediately shifted from our seats to his. As I patted Kristy's hand, I turned to look at Kai as well. I recognized him from student government; we've worked together a few times. He's always been a strong, smart, levelheaded kind of guy. In contrast to my friend, Kai was stoic. He had this odd hint of acceptance in his eyes like he had had a feeling all along he was going to be chosen. Maybe he had known. But the kid looked way too stable for someone who was just handed his dismal future.

"Brianna Barnett." When I heard my full name, I swear my lungs stopped working. Everything went fuzzy. Figures lost their outline, and the entire room went white. I must have made some sort of cry because Kristy suddenly wrapped her arms around me and hugged me to her. I gripped one of her arms with a vice-like grip. I can't even begin to describe the devastation I felt in my chest at that moment. I had a future, a plan. I have a family. How could they pick my name? Why my name? Why not someone else's name? The only comfort I had is Kristy will be traveling with me. We wouldn't be separated.

I was so caught up in my own feelings, I almost didn't hear the final name. The governor hesitated when he read it, much longer than any of the other names. He practically growled as he forced the words out between his teeth. "Ash Jackson." Now that name got the biggest reaction out of everyone. The governor's son was being sent to the Labyrinth. Ash leveled his eyes at his father with a blasé stare and grinned brightly. I felt unsettled seeing him so satisfied with being chosen. There's got to be a reason he was so elated, but I didn't have the time or the energy to contemplate it.

Everything moved so quickly from there. We only had three days to prepare for our government-accompanied departure. I left school and spent my remaining days with my family. We're really close, and my name being called was crushing to them. I don't think my mother stopped crying the entire three days. She even took off work! My mother never takes off work. She's Olivia Barnett, kickass lawyer to the stars. She's one of my biggest influences. She taught me to dream big and not to take no for an answer. Seeing her broken down like that was rough on me.

We invited the whole family in from all over the state, a whole host of grandparents, aunts, uncles, and cousins. My grandma spent hours giving me any kind of tip she could think of that might help me. "Don't let your guard down for a moment," she said. "Keep your eyes open at all times. Make sure you and your team sleep in shifts." The pit grew in my stomach more and more as she tried to give me lessons in how to use my water magic that I already knew. I didn't have the heart to tell her to stop, and I knew it made her feel better to have me run through all kinds of spells from creating streams, to making waves, and summoning typhoons with a flick of my finger. Well, that last one we didn't exactly run through; it's an illegal spell. But in the Labyrinth, it might be fair game, so it's important to know that it exists.

On my last night at home, my parents cooked a feast for us with all my favorites: Carolina barbecued pork, cornbread, corn on the cob, biscuits, and cherry cobbler. I ate my fill, for sure, until I could not get another forkful in my mouth. Did it exacerbate the churning anxiety in my stomach? Yes. Was it worth it, though? Absolutely. That night, no one talked of lessons to learn or tips to survive. Instead, we shared stories and favorite memories like it was any other Sunday night family reunion dinner. My little sister sat next to me the entire night and laid her head on my shoulder. I held her hand and stroked her hair lightly. I worry for her when I'm gone. I wish she could stay a kid a little longer and not worry about me. I hope the family doesn't rely on her too heavily to fill my place when I'm gone.

All too soon, we were off to the coast. We drove three hours to reach the docks where each individual family would see the four of us off. My parents held me close for a long time. I had a hard time letting go of them. My sister gripped my shirt so tightly that my father had to physically remove her hands from the fabric. The challengers boarded a boat manned by only a single driver and set our sights on the island out in the middle of the Atlantic Ocean. And now here we are. I look out over the endless sea in front of us, holding on to the rail around the edge to steady myself. I can't see anything but water for miles except one tiny blip of an island in the distance that we are racing towards. The bright sunny sky above us would be beautiful if we weren't headed towards the Labyrinth way too fast for my liking. I don't know if I'm ready for everything that comes next. Whatever that might be.

Looking at my teammates, I try to analyze them and their mental state. Kristy looks calm, but her white knuckles clench to the railing. Hopefully, her brain holds out. It's only occurring to me now that I may have to protect her myself. She's got no magic to aid her. Kai is sitting on a bench on the deck, one leg crossed over his knee talking quietly to Ash. His posture is rigid. On the surface, he might seem to be calm, but even his muscles are tight with apprehension. And Ash? Ugh. He's just leaning back against the rail without a care in the world. It takes everything in me not to douse him with seawater and shake him, screaming Don't you realize what we're heading into?

But I shouldn't. Not at the beginning like this. So I don't. I only watch the high ivy walls grow closer and closer to us as we speed forward towards our destiny.

4

Ash - Entering The Maze

When we finally reach the island where the Labyrinth is held, I breathe a sigh of relief. Unlike the other nervous faces around me, even Kai's, I'm not worried at all. Anywhere is better than home.

Especially after the days I've had. I'm lucky to have gotten out at all.

My parents were furious that I had filled out an application against their express orders. What's new? To me, this wasn't different from any other time I had done something my parents disapproved of. And they disapproved of a lot. Sometimes, small things like the wrong grade on a test they happened to find at the right time or big things like me getting caught at a party, wasted as fuck. But to them, this was the ultimate fuck you, the final straw. I was dreading coming home from school after my name was read. The look on my father's face was priceless, but furious. I stayed at Kai's for as long as I could and went home sometime past midnight.

But my parents were sitting up in the living room waiting for me. As soon as he saw me, my father just laid into me. He screamed in my face for a good hour about what a waste of space I was, how I was so selfish for even daring to stray from the path that they had set me on, and how furious he was that he couldn't stop it. That's the part of this whole thing that gave me strength: it was too late and the decision too high up in the ranks for the governor to fix. I was getting out, and there was nothing they could do. I stared right past him as he and my mother went back and forth with their anger and disappointment, internally smiling the whole time.

They ended up not speaking to me right up until I left. But when families were due to drop the challengers off at the docks, of course they came. Had to for the cameras. Wouldn't look good if the governor didn't accompany his own son as he was sent off to his potential death. Mom cried her fake tears, and my father turned on the fake emotions, giving a little speech to me (but really to the camera) about what it takes to be a man and how proud he is of me for stepping up. All complete bullshit, but at least I got a proper sendoff.

Our boat driver sends us from the edge of the shallow water to the beach in a little lifeboat. We float to shore while he speeds away. Dude's probably terrified to be this close to the source of all the world's problems.

The Ivy Labyrinth is stunning up close, a tall mass of ivy that winds together and shoots up to the sky. The walls stretch across the diameter of the island and circle around to an unseen point somewhere towards the south. As we disembark the lifeboat and climb up the small beach, I can feel the magical energy radiating off the maze. The smell is intoxicating. It draws me in, beckoning me closer. But at the same time, I'm intimidated by it, like I touch it, I'm going to disintegrate on the spot. I suppose it's possible that I might.

"Where do you think the entrance is?" the shy one, Kristy, speaks up. I don't think I've ever heard her voice before.

"The magic appears to be strongest just over this hill," Kai answers her. "I imagine that's where the entrance is."

Nodding in response to him, I pass the group and lead them up the hill. Brianna doesn't seem to like that much as she speeds up to match my stride. She's giving me this side-eye glare that I always notice her giving me whenever I pass by. I don't know what her problem is. I don't think I've ever talked to this girl, let alone done anything to make her hate me. Probably just another person caught up in the image of the troublemaker, Ash Jackson. Typical. I speed up to pass her as we come up on the entrance to the labyrinth.

Kai was right. The entrance is up here, and damn, is it kind of a letdown after seeing the majesty of the maze. I mean, it's beautiful, don't get me wrong. It's just a little… quiet. The entrance sits under a high sculpted arch of ivy and black roses. A magical barrier glows in the sunlight, showing a clear separation of outside vs. inside. Through the clear barrier, we can see down a long corridor adorned with trees and bushes that appear to turn to the left about a hundred yards in front of us. The opening looks pretty innocent, but who knows what could pop out once we step inside.

The four of us stand in front of the archway for several minutes, sort of observing it. Kristy walks around on either side of it and studies the wall a little more closely, even being so bold as to reach out and touch it. Part of me thinks I should stop her in case it sets something off, but honestly, I'm surprised she's brave enough to do so. To be fair, she is a mortal and doesn't exactly know the scale of how insane this much power concentrated here is. How she got chosen, I have no idea. Brianna stands in front of the entrance and stares down the corridor like she can somehow make it to the end without moving her feet. Kai watches over her shoulder from a ways back.

"This is ridiculous," I mumble to myself as I push past Brianna and step through the archway. Maybe not the smartest thing in the world, but it needed to be done. We were never going to get moving otherwise. Once I cross the threshold, I immediately feel a shift in my chest. I press back cautiously against the barrier I just stepped through and am instantly repelled. Instead of keeping me outside of the maze, now the barrier is keeping me in. I can never cross back out. My three classmates stare at me in shock.

"Dude," Kai laughs wryly. Brianna's jaw is practically on the ground, and Kristy stares at me like I have three heads.

"What? None of you were going to go."

"Yes, I was," Brianna scoffs at me. "I was coming up with a plan of what to do once we got inside. If you hadn't jumped the gun, I was about to share."

"Go ahead then."

She rolls her eyes. "No point now. We should have gone in together in case something was triggered. But obviously it wasn't." With that, she takes a large step over the barrier and strides past me, heading to the end of the corridor. I jog after her a bit while Kristy follows behind. Kai is the last to step through, and with that, we are officially trapped inside here for better or worse.

We walk down the long corridor-like forest. The trees hang down lower and lower over us until the entrance becomes a small object in the distance. The ivy appears to be about the same thickness along each of the walls, and when the sun hits it just right, you can see another magical barrier glittering above the top of the walls. There's no flying or climbing out. When we reach the edge of the corridor that feels just like walking through any forest at a park in town, suddenly the entire atmosphere changes. We are no longer in a discernible maze. Instead, we have been transported to a massive city.

"Oh my God," Brianna breathes.

Skyscrapers rise up all around us in silver and gold tinted glass. Interspersed randomly between are old wooden and brick houses and structures with genuine stores inside. The whole place is this weird hybrid between a modern city and something out of the Wild West in the 19th century. That's not even the strangest part. There's a whole mass of people standing in the streets and on the thresholds of buildings.

There are people here. I can't even begin to describe how shocked I feel seeing other beings inside of the Labyrinth. Unless they're holograms or an illusion.

The crowd parts, and instinctively, I throw a hand out in front of Brianna in hopes to keep the group behind me until we figure out what the hell is going on. She gives me a weird glance, but she seems to understand what I'm going for. She readies her hands, and I see a hint of blue water magic swirling in her hands. Oh, great. A naiad. Before I can reflect on what hell it's going to be like working with water magic and fire magic in the same group, an old gentleman walks out to meet us. He carries a long walking stick that thumps against the smooth dirt road with every step and wears a long purple robe that drags along the ground.

Looking directly at us, he says simply, "Welcome, challengers, to the Ivy Labyrinth."

5

Kai - The Rules

As we stand and stare at the city in front of us in silence, the older gentleman beckons us forward. "I imagine you all have a lot of questions. If you come to my office, I'll explain everything you need to know." The four of us look around at each other. Yeah, the whole thing feels like a trap, but there also doesn't seem to be any alternative but to move forward. I take the first step, and eventually, the others follow behind.

As we are led through the middle of town towards what appears to be some sort of town hall, I keep my eyes open and observe the landscape. The city's foundation is easy enough to understand. I sense a strong magical presence supporting each and every building that we pass by, similar to the magic used on the entrance to the Labyrinth. The city appears to be a direct creation of the maze itself, so although we are being welcomed with open arms, I'm still feeling wary. Mostly because I have no idea where all these people came from. I'm not convinced that some of them or all of them are not holograms.

I am unnerved by the people's stares. Men, women, and children watch us so carefully as we pass by. There's a mixture of joy and deep sadness in the crowd. A few people appear to be really excited to see us, but they stay silent and grant us small smiles. Others look upon us as they would a human sacrifice being offered to the gods. There are no claps or cheers like there were as we left home. Instead, I only feel a growing sense of dread building in my stomach. I try to ignore it as the group enters the tall brick town hall building.

After strolling through a marble-floored lobby, we are diverted into a large office. Two attendants wait on either side of the doors and pull them open for us. The walls are covered in wood paneling, and a simple set of four chairs that look like they've been pulled from someone's dining room sits in the center of the room in front of a heavy oak desk. The older gentleman takes a seat at the desk and beckons for all four of us to take a seat. Still hesitant, I take the first seat. The rest follow behind. To my left, Kristy looks around the room in awe, her mouth softly opening and closing with each new angle she turns her head.

"I apologize for the crowd," the man speaks in a steady, quiet voice. "Every time we have new challengers enter the Labyrinth, the maze sends out a major vibration. Everyone can feel it, and they almost always gather around the barrier between our city and the entrance. It's often overwhelming for people from the outside, so I hope you'll accept my apology on behalf of the city."

"Who are you?" Ash blurts out rudely. I shoot him an irritated glance, and he throws his hands up.

The older man smiles. "My name is Matthais Powers, and-"

"The Matthias Powers?" Kristy interrupts.

"Yes, miss. I suppose I am."

"I'm sorry, who is Matthias Powers?" Ash asks.

"He was one of the challengers for the Ivy Labyrinth from Canada's School of Werewolves and Sirens in Quebec. The application committee at the time was so impressed with his student leadership and athleticism that they put out stories in the press about how he was going to be the one who broke the Labyrinth's curse," Kristy gushes. "It's an honor to meet you, sir."

Matthias chuckles wryly. "Don't flatter me, child. I was a high school senior with an inflated ego only amplified by the press touting me and my team. We entered the maze, and we failed right away. Didn't even make it past the first challenge. So we ended up stuck here."

"Where is 'here', exactly?" Brianna finally speaks up for the first time since we entered the city.

"Welcome to Elvira, the city of the first fallen. Every person you see in this city is a challenger who failed the first obstacle that the Labyrinth threw at us. That is something important that you must understand - well, actually I think I'm getting ahead of myself. The Labyrinth has been very clear about the role of the Elder of Elvira, which is to give all new challengers the rules of the maze."

"The rules? There are actual rules?" Kristy blurts out.

Matthias frowns. "Yes, there are rules. Rules that are absolutely crucial for you to follow, or else you will fail and you will end up trapped like the rest of us. So please listen carefully." He takes a deep breath. "The first rule is the most important. The Labyrinth is an abstract location, so what I am about to tell you is not going to be anything like a set of directions or a map. Instead, I'm going to give you the basic nature of the maze. The most important thing for you to remember during any challenges you have to face is this: you must remain together at all times unless separated by the Labyrinth itself. That is rule number one. If you lose sight of each other, you will never be able to find each other again, and you will be stuck."

I look sideways at my companions. Ash looks a little more uneasy than when we started. Kristy is scribbling notes on a piece of paper she'd swiped off the Elder's desk. I chuckle lightly. So we're going to be together all the time, unable to separate too far from each other or we'll be trapped in a challenge. Great.

"The second rule," Matthias continues, "and possibly equally important to the first is that when the Labyrinth calls to you, you must go.

The call sounds different to each group, but trust me, you'll know it when you hear it. From what I can guess, there are multiple cities or towns throughout the Labyrinth for challengers to take a break, heal, or train. Those places are likely made up of people who got farther than my team and I did. Whatever challenge you fail, you will be transported to the closest settlement and… stay there."

"For how long?" Brianna asks tentatively like she already knows the answer to her question.

"Forever."

The tension in my body just floods out in one big rush of adrenaline. Matthias continues despite the obvious shock on all our faces. "Every person here is a failed challenger or the descendant of one."

"I'm sorry, the descendant of one?" Ash interrupts.

Matthias Powers nods. "After the first few decades, some of the challengers got together and became pregnant. When the children were born, the Labyrinth didn't seem to mind. But it turned out they couldn't leave any more than the rest of us could. The Labyrinth provides for everyone here reasonably well. Food, water, and all the buildings appeared one after the other as the Labyrinth adjusts to our needs and the challengers' needs. We live and work here like in any other society except for that we are on our own. No communication with the outside world and no communication with other cities in the Labyrinth."

He sighs quietly. "I am sorry to dump all of this on you so soon. However, you'll need the information to move forward."

"When do we move forward?" I ask. Kristy glances over at me quickly like she's surprised that I was behind her.

"Could be a day. Could be two," the Elder replies. "The timeline is never consistent. You'll find that the Labyrinth will control every waking moment. Every sleeping moment too. In the meantime, while you wait, my men will escort you to a guest house where you can stay in the meantime. You'll find a training center attached for you to practice any magical or physical skills you may need when you encounter your first challenge."

"What is the first challenge?" Ash interrupts.

Matthias smiles sadly. "I am not allowed to disclose that. I couldn't even if I wanted to; there is magic in play to keep me from assisting you further." He rises to his feet and reaches out his hand. "Good luck to you all." I'm the first to take it, shaking it firmly. The others follow suit. The office doors reopen, and we are swiftly escorted outside and towards the guest house, reeling from the news.

6

Brianna - Attempts Were Made

When we arrive at the guest house, I'm trying to process what the fuck just happened in that room. Not only are we finding out that everyone who ever entered the Labyrinth is trapped forever somewhere inside, but now we're realizing that we have to stay together the entire time, all up in each other's personal space. Or, we could be stuck in a challenge and potentially die. I'm freaking out. Death is almost more appealing than a lifetime of imprisonment in a magical trap. I was prepared to die, but to live forever here? To never see my family again but know that they are out there, waiting for me forever?

No way.

I try to keep my breath steady and even as the attendants leave us alone in the guest house. I don't want the others to know how much I'm freaking out. The house is tiny, but open. There's a living room and a decent-sized kitchen with a small fridge. I spot a couple of bedrooms along the back of the house with two beds each. Ash plops himself right down on the couch and lays across it with a big stretch. Kristy takes one of the comfy chairs while Kai heads to the kitchen to inspect if anything is in the fridge. He brings us a few bottles of water and sets them on the glass coffee table before sitting down himself. I decide to remain leaning against the wall. I'm afraid if I sit down, I may never get back up.

Surprisingly, Kristy is the first to speak up. "I think we need to take stock of what we have to work with."

"What do you mean?" Kai asks her.

A soft pink blush spreads across my friend's face, the same one she gets when she's trying to communicate an idea she has in her head without embarrassing herself. "I think we need to compile what kinds of skills each of us can contribute. It's not like we hang out all the time and know a lot about each other."

"What are you talking about?" Ash interjects roughly, as if Kristy has some big secret that she isn't sharing with us. He's got his hands locked together in his lap and his face is screwed up in confusion. I cringe. When Kristy is asked to elaborate, she can sometimes fumble.

I'm proud when she continues as though she was never interrupted. "Look, you're all magical, right? Kai is a dragon shapeshifter, and Ash is an elemental Fae. Both of you have fire magic. Brianna is a naiad and has water magic. That's the basic gist of it, but can you give me more specifics?"

When the boys don't answer right away, I take the lead. "I can summon water from the earth no matter the distance from the surface. I can manipulate the ocean, rivers, lakes, and freeze water. I haven't used my magic to freeze anything wider than a stream, but I imagine it's not too difficult. Oh, I can summon and manipulate storms if necessary, but it's an extremely complicated form of magic. And when I'm in the water, I also have a naiad form I can shift into, but I haven't done it in a while."

Kai understands the question now and chimes in. "I'm good with any form of fire magic: fireballs, fire summoning, fire manipulation, and a little bit of work with lightning. I can shift to a full blown dragon and fly both in and out of that shift. It also gives me some type of super strength and speed in certain situations. Occasionally some wind manipulation with the flight. Those powers can be difficult to trigger. I almost always have to be in dragon form."

Ash shrugs. "Basically the same as Kai minus the dragon, the wind, and the lightning." Kristy chuckles. "The fire aspects are the same. Though mine are a little more refined than his. More precise, fancier, etcetera."

Kai rolls his eyes at his friend. "Likely story."

"You wanna test that right now?" Ash leaps to his feet. "There's a training center somewhere behind this place, right?" Despite Kristy attempting to interrupt in protest, he darts off towards the back door. Kai takes off after him. With a heavy sigh and a pointed look at each other, Kristy and I follow behind.

We pass through a breezeway at the back of the house to get to the attached training center. The windows allow me to catch another glimpse of the city. The buildings glitter in the afternoon sunlight. I wonder if the sun is the one from the outside world or if the Labyrinth created its own sun. From what I've seen so far, it wouldn't be that surprising.

The training center is pretty big, to my surprise. It's a little dusty from lack of use, but there's no lack of resources inside. There are plenty of mats for us to train on and a variety of weights and exercise equipment. Kristy trails her fingers over a set of uneven bars while my attention is drawn to the swords along the wall. Damn, aren't they beautiful? I pull one off the wall. It's a good-sized blade, a little larger than the ones Kristy and I use on our fencing team. I beckon for Kristy to come over and take a look while Ash and Kai wrestle with each other. She grimaces at the sword in my hands. "Are you sure you want to use something like that? It's not like fencing. Those are medieval weapons."

"Don't be silly, Kris," I wave off her concerns. "It can't be that different. Just a little bigger and heavier. Besides, I have to learn and improve somehow, right?" I hold the sword out and do a couple practice swings before walking over to one of the mats and sitting down to study it. Ash and Kai eventually stop wrestling, and Ash moves over to the rack to pick up a blade himself. He's holding it all wrong, and his practice swings are clumsy. He's got no idea what he's doing.

I call out and ask him, ""Do you have any idea what you're doing?"

"Sure," he snarks back. "It's a sword. You swing things, and you piss people off." His tone is sick with sarcasm.

"You're not holding it right. You're going to make yourself a bigger target for someone trying to attack you because they can see you can't fight with one, and you're going to hurt yourself in the process. At least try to be a little less sloppy."

Ash shoots me a surprised look. "What makes you an expert in swords?"

"I took fencing for years. I'm one of the strongest competitors on the team. I place almost every time."

He gives a little shrug and turns his attention to my friend. "Hey Kristy. What kind of talents are you bringing to the table, exactly? You're a mortal chick. How do you expect to keep up with the rest of us?"

"Hey," Kai warns him.

I open my mouth to retort, but Kristy speaks first. "I may not have magic, but I bet I can outsmart either of you. I have book smarts and knowledge of ancient and magical languages. Have you even studied the spells that you use? Or do you just try things and hope they work out? On top of that, I have gymnastics training and fencing, like Brianna. I may not do well in a magical fight, but I bet I could hold my own in a physical one."

Ash holds his hands up. "Alright, alright. Just don't slow us down." He swings the blade in a ridiculously incorrect manner, which is honestly starting to piss me off. Kristy sees that I'm boiling and steps in.

"Bri, why don't you and I try these out?" She grips the sword in her hand and gives me a playful smirk that she usually only gives me when we're alone.

I grin back and shrug casually. "Alright. You're on." I love a good fight, and I know Kristy wants to prove herself. We walk towards the mats in the middle of the room, and I raise my sword up in the air. Without another word, Kristy bursts forward and swings her sword at my head. My heart skips a beat as she narrowly misses me. So that's how she wants to do it. I swing my own sword at her waist, and she steps back as it passes in front of her. We cross swords in an X formation before I jerk away from her and drop low to create some distance between us. She crosses her sword with mine again. Ash and Kai stop fooling around and move closer to get a better look at our fight.

These blades may be different than what I'm used to, but I quickly fall back into a familiar pattern. We step forward and move back to collide over and over again. "She's pretty fast," Kai whistles in approval. Ash grunts in agreement.

Kristy grins. "I may not be stronger than her, but I can outsmart her."

My focus sharpens, and a smirk crosses my lips. "You're right. I'm not so smart." I let her believe her little comment for a moment, only to take advantage of it. When I come at her from the side, she thinks it's a misstep and swings her sword at me. I dive underneath the blow and grab her ankles, yanking her to the ground. I point my blade above her throat and grin. "Who's the smart one now?"

Her smile beams back at me. "Still me." With lightning-quick reflexes, she rolls out from under me and leaps to her feet. When she swings at me, I duck under the blade and grab my own sword to bat hers away. We both collect ourselves as we circle each other. This girl is just as much of a spitfire as I am. But I'm in for a hell of a surprise when she hauls off and kicks at my sword hand. My blade goes flying across the room, and she presses the blade to my chest. "Checkmate."

I breathe heavily as Kai and Ash clap. "Damn," Kai breathes.

Ash smirks. "Guess you can hold your own as a mortal. But Brianna, damn. What does it say about you getting your ass kicked by a mortal?"

I growl in rage. He still doesn't get it. Before I can lunge at his face, Kristy grabs my arm and pulls me towards the guest house.

"Shut up, Ash," she says as she leads me back towards the house. I don't even protest as I let her drag me along. I swear, I'm going to strangle him with my bare hands before we get through this Labyrinth.

7

Kristy - Into The Unknown

After a long night of keeping Brianna from ripping Ash apart, I wake to a heavy vibration and ringing in my ears. It's an unfamiliar foreboding kind of sound that presses in on either side of my head. I cover my ears, but the sound doesn't dampen. When I look over to the bed on the opposite wall, I see Brianna sitting up and covering her ears too. "What is that?" she asks me, shouting over the din.

"I don't know!" I shout back.

A loud banging comes at the bedroom door. "Hey!" Kai calls through the wood. "Can you hear that?"

It occurs to me then what the sound is. "Y'all, I think it's the Labyrinth. I think this is it." I scramble out of bed and rush to grab a change of clothes. "We need to get dressed now and head out."

"Head out where?" Brianna's voice grows slowly more panicked with each word as she rolls out of bed and reaches for her bag.

"Wherever we're supposed to go." As I slip on my shirt, I contemplate my own answer. I have no idea where we are supposed to go. Will it become obvious once we step outside the guest house? Will there be something like a beam of light shining down on where we are supposed to be? Or do we have to follow the sound (which is still ringing in my ears, by the way) until we find where to start like some irritating game of hot and cold?

Brianna and I step out into the living room where Kai and Ash are already waiting. "Took you long enough," Ash scoffs.

"Good morning to you too," I snap back. What is this guy's problem?

"Sorry," Kai smiles at me. "He's not a morning person." I nod and give him a little smile back. Kai has a nice smile. It's the perfect size for his face and gives him little dimples. Not that I'm paying that much attention to it.

I look down and spot a set of backpacks on the table. "What are those?"

"The Elder's attendants dropped off some supplies for us. There's a tent and food and a few hand tools and weapons. I saw a few other things inside, but I didn't want to unpack everything and repack. But it looks like we'll be set wherever we're going, at least for a while." Kai winces and shouts a little louder. "We need to leave. The ringing is getting worse."

"Yeah," I agree with him and snatch one of the backpacks off the table. "Let's get going." The others each pick up a bag, and I lead the way out the door.

As soon as I step through the door, the bright morning sky is snatched away from us like someone removed a tablecloth from a table. It folds in on itself as it is pulled away and replaced with nothing but darkness. The guest house's front steps shift forward and become a smooth ramp under our feet. I try to warn the others, but before I can open my mouth, the ramp tips us down and we tumble into the blackness. I let out a shriek as I fall.

This is my worst nightmare. I can't see or hear anything except that damn intense ringing that seems to be growing to a crescendo in my ears. I tumble further and further down into the darkness. It swallows me up, and I am powerless against it. I kick and struggle as the Labyrinth's magic drags me down. My wrists suddenly snap together, pulled by an unseeable force, and I collide with a hard surface.

Not with the ground, as I first suspected. I soon realize I hit a chair. A single light above our heads flashes on abruptly, and I find myself sitting in an upright chair handcuffed to Kai behind me. Brianna and Ash are cuffed beside us in a similar formation. The light reflects around us through four mirrors placed in a diamond formation. Each of us is framed in one of the reflections. Above mine reads a singular inscription: Your differences will either save you or be your demise.

Immediately, my panic shuts off. It's a puzzle, a riddle to solve. That's my specialty; I love to solve puzzles. I don't need to be afraid of the darkness anymore. I just need to concentrate. As I look around, I catch a glimpse of Brianna beside me. Her eyes are wide, and she struggles against the handcuffs attaching her to Ash. He swears at her. "Dammit Brianna, hold still. You're yanking at my wrists." Despite his protest, she keeps moving. He grips three of her fingers tightly in his hand and squeezes hard. She yelps. "I said stop!"

"Calm down guys," Kai's voice comes just behind my ear. "Seriously. Let's figure this out." I feel him shifting behind me, his back grazing against mine as he turns to scan as much of the room as he can. "What are we looking at?"

"Are there any inscriptions on the other mirrors?" I ask.

"I don't see any. Do you have one?"

"Yes. It says your differences will either save you or be your demise. I think it's some sort of riddle."

"What do you think it means?" Ash struggles lightly against the chair he's in. Out of the corner of my eye, I watch him take stock of the four of us and our captured state. I find it interesting how Kai jumped right into observing the scene while Ash took an extra moment to check on the rest of us. I wouldn't have expected that from him.

But I'm getting distracted. I need to focus on the task at hand. "Okay...

the mirrors are important. We need to look at ourselves and each other to figure out how we differ." I turn to study myself in the mirror. "Let's start with the physical. Call out hair and eye colors."

"Why? Can't you remember?" Ash snaps.

"I need to hear them out loud to absorb them properly," I clap back. "Now tell me."

Ash begrudgingly answers, "White hair, blue eyes."

"Brown hair, green eyes," Brianna chimes in.

"Brown hair, hazel eyes," Kai says behind me.

"Brown hair, blue eyes," I whisper quietly to myself. My brain works to put together and unscramble the letters in hopes to find some sort of message hidden inside. But the pieces aren't coming together. "Are you sure there aren't any other inscriptions on those mirrors?"

Brianna narrows her eyes at the one in front of her. "No inscriptions, but mine has two short series of numbers and letters on the side. 1, equals sign, C and then 2, arrow sign, V."

"So there is more to this," I mumble to myself. "Kai, Ash, do you see any other symbols anywhere?"

"I just have one massive arrow pointed down to the floor on the left side." Kai answers.

"I have four elemental symbols on the four corners of the glass," Ash adds.

With that, everything clicks for me. "We were missing type."

"Type?"

I grin brightly. "Yes. Mortal, naiad, dragon shapeshifter, elemental Fae. Brianna's mirror says take the first consonant of each word, the second letter if it's a vowel. Differences with the mirrors doesn't mean physical; the elemental symbols represent each type that we are. The mirrors are meant to both open our eyes and be misleading." The puzzle's so clever, I'm practically fangirling over here at its brilliance. "The letters are m, o, n, a, d, and e. The arrow pointing down..." I look up directly into the mirror. "It's daemon. Divinity between god and human."

With a sudden jerk, the chairs fly apart to separate. Brianna shrieks. The handcuffs break and disappear off our wrists. Before we can process anything, the floor opens up under us and we tumble down, down, down into the unknown.

8

Ash - The Elemental Chambers

As we fall through the floor for the second time today, I'm getting more irritated. If I wanted to be thrown around like a rag doll, I would hit the pool with the baseball team during one of Kai's weekend parties. At least this time, we can see a stark white tile floor rising towards us as we tumble. We hit the ground, palms and knees first. Mine ache at the impact. The magic of the Labyrinth doesn't seem to be deliberately intending to harm us, or else the sheer momentum of our falls would be obeying the laws of physics and breaking limbs at the very least. But it definitely could be a lot gentler.

I'm the first to get up off the ground and take stock of this next room. The room is almost entirely made of glass and white tile. As opposed to the first room that was mostly in darkness, there is so much light in here that it's almost blinding. We stand in a narrow pathway surrounded by four separate chambers separated by glass. Looking up from where we fell, all I see is a tiled ceiling. There's no evidence of the place we just were. However, I do spot where we are supposed to go next, a small platform with a big iron door. That must be our exit.

Brianna pulls Kristy up and joins me in looking around the room. "At least we can see in this one," she says. "Any ideas, Kristy?"

"Give me a minute…" She turns around slowly while looking up. I shift to face her and wait for her to think as well. She was right about the mirrors, and it was pretty impressive how fast she figured it out. Can't deny she's got a decent head on her shoulders. "There's some type of platform up there," she muses. "To reach it, I'm guessing we need to deal with the chambers."

"Do you see any markings in them?" Kai moves behind Kristy to look over her shoulder.

"Yeah. Look at the squares with the railings." The four of us move closer to the glass. Inside each of the vertical chambers is a large raised square platform in the center with a carving of one of the four elements: a flame for fire, a wave for water, a gust of wind for air, and a coarse stone for earth. The platform has rails on either side, and in front of each platform sits a small table, almost like an altar. There are no buttons or any indication of what we are supposed to do.

"One chamber for each of us," I say as I move towards one of the doors.

Kai grabs my arm and pulls me back. "Hey, don't go charging in again. Let's just wait for a sec." Brianna lets out a soft chuckle, which pisses me off. Does she plan to make a little sound or comment at everything I say or do?

I throw my hands up. "Fine, fine. I'll wait."

Kristy turns to the group. "Okay, Ash should take the fire chamber. Kai, you should take the air chamber because of the whole dragon thing. Brianna, water obviously. And I'll take earth. That's what makes the most sense."

"What happens once we're in there?" Brianna asks.

"I don't know," her friend replies. "But I have a feeling those doors will be sealed. We'll have to figure out what each chamber wants before we can get to the exit."

"So in other words, we're going in blind," I say bluntly.

"Yeah. But we don't really have a choice, so I don't think your comment is necessary or helpful." I resist the urge to laugh. Kristy can glare all she wants, but her size and face lack the bite of a good menacing stare.

"Now can I go in?" I ask. She nods and waves me off. Swinging open the glass door, I step inside the chamber and let the door close. Kristy predicted correctly; the door disappears as soon as it closes. She's got a good instinct for this stuff. I watch my companions enter their own chambers and each of the doors vanish one by one. "Hello?" I call out tentatively. "Can you guys hear me at all?"

Kai is quick to reply. "Yeah. I can hear you. Your voice is faint, but we should be able to communicate with each other if we shout. You guys hear okay?"

"Yes!"

"Heard you fine!"

Once we confirm that we're all okay, parchment pops up on each of the tables. Kristy's table also adds a series of irregularly shaped stones while Ash's adds a series of white crystals. She seems startled by it in the earth chamber next to mine, but I'm not phased. Things keep popping in and out of this maze, and we might as well start getting used to it. I lean over my table and read the parchment. Each chamber's task must be completed simultaneously for the platforms to rise.

"Do you all have the thing about needing to complete the tasks at the same time?" I call out to confirm.

"Yeah!" I get three yeses one right after the other.

"What's the plan then?"

"We put together whatever we need to put together first and leave the last step or component for coordinating our approach to the altar," Kristy offers the plan. I nod in agreement.

"Let's do it then." I turn to the rest of my parchment and read the next set of lines. Fire chamber: build a pyramid of flame, brick by brick, on the altar table. That seems like a bit of an oddly specific request. A pyramid of flame is easy, just a basic shape. I can cast that in my sleep. I have before, actually. You never want to be around me if I have a nightmare. It's like all the safeguards go down on my power and my magic just lashes out. My parents eventually had to hire a Fae friend of theirs to put a protection spell on my room to keep me from absolutely destroying the house.

Brick by brick. In flame. You only build something brick by brick when you want people to stop and admire the work. You want something sturdy, but beautiful. Something that when people walk by, they can't help but stop and stare at it for a long time and admire its craftsmanship. I don't do that. I don't do intricate things; I do whatever gets the job done quickest and easiest.

When I glance around to the other chambers, the task appears to be the same for everyone based on their element. Kai is lifting each crystal delicately with a soft breeze emanating from his hands. The way his base looks through the glass, it looks like he is holding each crystal together by manipulating the air in between them. He's a powerful guy, but that's going to be exhausting after a while.

Brianna… I'm not a fan of water magic, don't get me wrong. Fire mages are schooled from birth to stay away from water mages at all costs. But I can't deny how pretty it looks when she forms soft water beads by drawing them out of one of the water thermoses stored in her pack. She coaxes them out one at a time and sets them one on top of the other. They look so solid, you could just reach out and touch them.

And Kristy? Kristy's holding her own. She's found a pocket knife in a zippered pouch and is hand-sanding down the stones so they'll fit together.

Which probably means I should start on my task. All it takes is a flick of my fingers to generate a tiny flame. I grin as I let it roll down my fingertips and across the back of my hand. I love playing with magic.

It's a real rush to feel all that power below the surface of your skin. I let the first flame fall to the table and sit there. With another flick, I add two more flames next to it. It takes a certain amount of concentration to make sure they remain separate entities. I create a wide base before stacking upward, increasing the amount of power that I'm using to hold everything together.

When I reach the top, I call out to the others. "Hey! Where are we at? Is everyone ready?"

"Ready over here," Kristy calls back.

"Ready." Kai's gruff, tired voice answers next.

"Me too," Brianna finally closes out.

"Who wants to count it down?"

"I will," Brianna replies again, locking eyes with me. I nod to her. "Alright! Three… two… one… now!"

I set my final flame on top of my pyramid, and the altar suddenly descends partially into the floor. A flick of my eyes around the room assures me that this has happened in all of the other chambers. The glass around the chambers falls around us and vanishes. With a jerk, the platform I'm standing on begins to rise towards the ceiling. I grab onto the railing in surprise. Kristy is gripping her railing with a deathlike grasp. Wonder if she's scared of flying.

Each of the four platforms moves towards the ceiling and locks in place against one another to form a railed bridge. I offer Kristy my hand, and she holds it tightly. Behind me, Kai helps Brianna over. We walk over carefully to the platform with the door. We all crowd in close to avoid falling off the back. Kai keeps to the outside. I suppose if he falls, he can catch himself better than the rest of us can.

With a deep breath, Kristy grips the door handle and pushes it open. We walk through, one behind the other. I'm hoping this is the exit. Though knowing the Labyrinth, we're nowhere near done with this challenge sequence.

9

Brianna - Fighting Our Way Out

This is exhausting.

I am tired of the Labyrinth throwing us around. It's not enough for the maze to test our convictions and our skills by putting us through this fast-paced environment; the magic also has to toss us every which way on top of it. It's irritating, and I'm not enjoying it.

Although the door to the third room was close to the ceiling, the group of us enter on the ground again. Oddly, we are also outside. Or some semblance of outside. There is grass and dirt under our feet, leading to a tall rock formation that rises up in a winding ramp to another door that sort of hovers in the air. Although there appears to be a blue sky, I can see the shimmering of a magical barrier only a few dozen feet up. This is definitely a room; it has boundaries and edges. As much as the Labyrinth tries to trick the eye with grass that seems to stretch on for miles and a sky that goes up endlessly, we are no more out in the open than we were at any other point in our journey.

As I take a few steps away from the group, a loud pop startles me. A rack of fencing weaponry appears on my right. I immediately freeze where I am. "Nobody move," I order quietly.

"What?" Ash, who is closest to me, stops and shifts forward slightly.

I throw a hand up fast. "Stop!" Kai and Kristy turn to look at me. "Nobody move," I repeat.

"What's the problem, Bri?" Kristy asks.

I point to the rack of swords. "Did you guys see that pop in?"

"No," Ash replies. "What happened?"

"When we walked into the room, that rack wasn't there. I took a few steps forward, and it appeared out of nowhere. I think the floor may have magical triggers."

"That would make sense," Kristy nods in agreement. "All the other rooms had some sort of trigger to escape. The mirror room needed the code word to be said, and the glass room required the elements to work together at the same time. This time, maybe our presence is the trigger for some sort of event. A fencing event, maybe?"

"There's gonna be a fight," I conclude. I turn to Kai and Ash. "Y'all can't really handle a sword, can you?"

"No," Ash answers. "But I'm good with fire." He throws out his hand, presumably to do some sort of attack flame. But nothing comes out. A look of panic flashes over his face as he repeats the hand motion. When he gets the same result, he curses loudly. "Kai!" he shouts. "What the hell?"

Kai flicks his own fingers to no avail. "Alright, that's strange," he says, albeit much more calmly than his friend.

"Brianna, try yours," Kristy urges. Just as I suspected, my magic is out too.

"Alright then," I groan. "Looks like magic is out of the question. Gotta be some kind of magic dampening spell. Swords only then."

"This is ridiculous!" Ash throws his hands up and stomps forward two steps.

"Don't!" Kristy and I shout at the same time.

But it's too late. When he takes a third step, I hear a distinctive click echo from under his feet. At the bottom of the rock face, a series of stones stacked on top of each other slowly slides open. I swear under my breath as a silver knight steps out of the chamber. He is tall, broad, and holds a foil in his right hand. He turns sharply and starts to move to the right, and a second knight comes out to his previous place. He turns left, and a third appears. This continues until eight knights block the entrance to the ramp leading to the exit.

Within a breath, suddenly the knights are charging at us. The four of us scatter. I make a beeline for the sword rack. Thank the powers that be that they are sabers. Kristy and I know saber fencing like the backs of our hands. I grab two in each hand and rush back to Kristy. I pass off the saber to her. She grins. "Thanks, Bri." Seemingly unafraid, she charges at the nearest knight and clashes blades with him.

I don't stick around to see how she fares. Instead, I dodge my way around two knights to shove the weapon into Kai's hands. Luckily, Ash makes his way over to where I am so I don't have to go running to him. "We don't have a lot of time. Hold the sabre like this." I demonstrate for them. "Thumb along the backstrap of the grip, index finger around to meet the knuckle of your thumb. Pinch to keep it steady. Three fingers in a light wrap around." Both of them pick up the grip fairly quickly. "Good. Now move your asses and get to the door."

Without another word, I charge into the crowd of automated knights to give Kristy some assistance. Slashing forward, my blade collides with one of theirs. The knight doesn't fight like a fencer. It's much wilder than that, swinging every which way and moving however it wants to. That means I don't have to stick to fencing rules either. I dance around this knight and stab it through the chest. The metal is surprisingly pliant; the saber sinks right in. But to my surprise, the knight doesn't fall; it only falters.

I dodge another swing over my head. Something tells me that if I get hit by one of these blades, I will be injured. I spin around to the other side of the robot and stab it through the back. This time, the thing sparks and freezes before crashing to the ground. "Stab them in the back!" I shout before getting to work on another knight.

"Like a video game?" Kai calls back.

I glance over my shoulder and shoot him a puzzled grin. Who knew star athlete boy was a gamer? "Yeah!" I shout back while making quick work of my opponent. When it falls to the ground, I rush towards the open entrance to the winding ramp.

Out of the corner of my eye, I watch Ash fall to the ground, knocked over by one of the aggressors. His arm shows a thin red line below his sleeve where he got sliced. Blood bubbles to the surface sluggishly. As the knight draws his saber back to stab Ash in the chest, I rush to counter it. I block the move and spin around to the knight's back to stab it. As it falls to its knees, I grip Ash's hand and yank him to his feet. "You're welcome." I flick my head towards the ramp. "Let's go. Let's go!" I shout to the others. Kristy and Kai get the message and abandon the remaining knights. We rush the ramp together and wind our way up.

Near the top just before we reach the door, I am startled when one of the knights hurls a saber at my feet. I'm too late to stop in front of it while running, and I trip. My body angles right, and I tumble off the edge of the rock face. I let out a shriek, reaching for the lip to hold on. Ash's hand launches out and grabs my right hand. My arm jerks nearly out of my socket as I am held up by his grip. Kai grabs my left hand and pulls me back onto the pathway. I breathe heavily and grip both of the boys' hands tightly as I lean forward away from the edge.

Fuck. I almost died. What the hell? With a gulp, I look up at Ash who is staring at me with an indiscernible expression. "You're welcome," he says shortly.

Embarrassed to have my own language used against me, I brush past him carefully and yank the next door open. With a deep breath, I charge inside. I need to put space between me and that infuriating… albeit somewhat helpful boy.

10

Kai - Don't Let Her Fall

I feel kinda useless in the maze right now.

We're moving quickly through this first series of rooms, but I feel like I haven't really helped much. Kristy solved that first puzzle so fast. Sure, I was useful in the elemental chamber, but using such a concentrated form of magic took a lot out of me. I'm an athlete. That's my major skill in life. Okay, maybe that's not entirely true, but that's what it feels like sometimes. I'm not as quick-witted as some of the others; it takes me a little more time to process information. I have never been pushed hard enough to improve on that. My parents took so much time to focus on athletics, they weren't exactly paying attention to my brain. I had decent grades, but frankly, they didn't give a damn whether they were good or mediocre.

I think I'm about to get my lucky break though as we enter the new room. Or a better word for it would be a platform. The four of us stand suspended a few dozen feet off the ground on a railed wooden rectangle. A steady wind blows at us from behind. In front of us lies a high ropes course with multiple elements that extend somewhere out in the distance. If I squint my eyes, I can see another platform in the distance marking the end of the course.

"Woah," Brianna breathes with an admiring smile. "This is awesome."

Ash whistles. "Finally, something we can run through easy."

As I look across the course, I notice out of the corner of my eye that Kristy doesn't seem to be as thrilled as the rest of us. She stands very still, definitely the least amount of movement that I have seen from her since we started. I don't have much time to dwell on it though as we are startled by the sudden appearance of four harnesses and associated clips at our feet. "Here we go then," Ash cheers as he picks up and attaches a harness to his body. The rest of us do the same. The familiar weight settles onto me, and I grin. I can't wait to get out there.

Brianna is the first to hook her clip to the top line and start working her way across the first stretch of rope towards a Z-shaped balance beam a little ways out. Ash quickly follows behind. "Hey!" he shouts at her. "Wait up!" She just laughs and starts moving faster. Before long, the two of them were engaged in a half-race, half-shoving match as they began to traipse their way across the boards.

I chuckle as I hook up my own clip. I take a few steps out into the air, grinning at the feeling of the wind moving over me. Ropes courses are one of my guilty pleasures. Every winter break, my family and I go skiing in the Blue Mountains up in Pennsylvania. It's gorgeous during that time of year, and the resort that we usually stay at has several types of ropes courses that we love to challenge each other on. My father likes to time my older brothers and me and compare our fastest times. It becomes like a week-long competition, and my family is seriously competitive. It gets crazy.

I climb across almost to the first obstacle before turning back to the platform to check on Kristy's progress. She is frozen, paralyzed at the railing. She hasn't moved an inch since we first came into this challenge. Concerned, I make my way back to the platform, unclip, and step onto it. "Hey… are you okay?" Now that I am closer, I can see that she is in a full-blown panic. She is very quiet, and her breath is super shallow.

Her hands vibrate lightly at her sides, and she stares off into space like she's not seeing me. When I touch her arm, she jumps violently. I have to catch her by taking both of her arms. "Hey... it's just me."

"Hi," she blurts out awkwardly. Her face flushes.

"Hi," I smile softly at her. "You okay?"

She hesitates, and her eyes avoid mine like she's about to lie. I wait patiently for her to talk, and eventually, she decides against it. "I'm afraid of heights."

"Ah," I sigh.

"We're gonna fail," she laughs dryly. "We're going to fail right here, and it's going to be my fault." She laughs louder this time with a hint of pain at the end as she drops her head to stare at her feet.

"That bad, huh?" I say as I let go of her arms. As soon as the words are out of my mouth, I cringe. That couldn't have been more wrong to say right then. *Of course it's that bad. Come on, Kai. Don't be a dumbass.*

Luckily, she doesn't seem to be too phased by my fuckup. "Yeah. I've never been able to do high ropes courses. I have panic attacks on airplanes and even mountain hikes. There's no way."

I nod slowly as I try to come up with a plan. We have to work our way across this course. Brianna and Ash are probably already at the end wondering what happened to us. But Kristy can't move. "Okay... Okay, what about if I help you across?"

"What?" Kristy looks up at me incredulously. "What do you mean?"

"I'll walk with you. We can make our way across together. You can grip my hand whenever you need help. We'll go slow."

"Are you sure?"

"Yeah."

She looks over at me and then the course before taking a shaky breath. She finally nods once. "Okay. I'll try."

"Good." I re-clip my hook to the top line and offer my hand to her. She takes it cautiously, and I clip her hook right next to mine. "Alright, grip onto the cords here with one hand. Hold on tight. It'll help anchor you and your brain once we're out there. That's how my mom got over her fear of climbing." Kristy immediately tightens her hold on them. I smile reassuringly. "Good. That's good. Let's go."

I lead her out onto the course one step at a time. We move sideways carefully. Kristy tries to keep her eyes clenched closed, but I tap her on the shoulder. "No, no, keep your eyes open and look out. Look towards where we're going. Don't look down. Keep your eye on the destination." Slowly, she opens her eyes. They start to drift downwards, but I catch her chin. "No. Look at me." Then she keeps her eyes locked to mine, and I feel strange. I've never had someone look at me with such need, such desperation. It's becoming clear to me that the only reason she is trying to do this is because I am standing here with her. I don't want to let her down. This, I can do. This, I can help her with.

When we reach the Z-shaped balance beam, I pause for a moment. "Okay, we're gonna step on these beams now. They might wobble a bit. Feel free to grab my arm. It changes direction every four feet or so. There are six of them. You got it?"

"Yeah," she sighs. "I got it." She seems a little more determined now. The longer I get to know her, I'm learning that she's actually quite tough. I wonder why I never noticed that before. To be fair, I only ever saw her intermittently in the hallway between classes. She used to blend into the crowd so easily. I don't know what's changed.

When we step on the first board, it sways a bit. She reaches out and grabs my arm with a vice-like grip. I pat her hand and talk to her as we move across the boards. "I used to do these courses a lot with my family."

"Really?" she breathes out in a rush.

"Yes. Every winter, we go skiing up north in Pennsylvania."

"Blue Mountains?" she asks.

"Yeah. How did you guess?"

She chuckles breathily. "My father grew up there. It's one of his favorite places to visit."

"That's great. But yeah, there's this resort that we always stay at, and one of their recreation options is a series of high ropes courses in different difficulties."

"Who is choosing to do that on their vacation?"

I laugh loudly. "Our family is. I have two older brothers, Marius and Robin, and we used to chase each other all over the elements. We tried to do all six courses in a row on the same day and race each other. They're working out in the world now, but they can usually take a few days off to join us in the mountains. We still race on them regularly." I lean in close to her ear. "One time, I pushed Robin off balance on the zipline, and he got stuck in the middle for a good half hour. The attendants couldn't figure out how to get him down. He was terrible at swinging his legs." Kristy almost doubles over laughing, and I feel proud of thinking of a good enough distraction.

The cargo net element goes much smoother. Kristy likes having something solid under her hands and feet. Though she holds on a little too tight when the wind blew through the net and made it sway. I have to pry her fingers off of the rope and help her to move through once more. The pipe bridge goes alright too. Kristy has got some serious flexibility. She didn't even fumble between logs as she stretched her leg out to step on each one. I'm kinda impressed.

But when we reach the end zipline, she tenses up again. The line is admittedly pretty steep and looks to be at a hell of a lot sharper angle than it actually is. "Kai, I can't," she pleads. "I can't. I'm gonna fall."

"You are not gonna fall." I grip her arm firmly and force her to look at me. "You're just gonna fly for a while. The platform is just down there. The exit is on the other side. See Brianna?" She narrows her eyes at the platform down in front of us a little ways off. A female figure waves at us. "She's gonna catch you."

"What if I fall?"

"I'll catch you."

Her eyes blink fast in confusion. "You're going to catch me?"

I smile teasingly at her. "Dragon, remember?" She blushes again and laughs. I'm finding that I like her laugh. "Okay, are you ready?"

"No. But I can be." She grants me a small smile, and I pat her arm again.

"Alright. Close your eyes." She shuts them tightly. "I'm gonna give you a little push, okay?" She nods fast. With a gentle hand to her back, I give her a soft shove. She squeals as she goes soaring down the line. I see that she opens her eyes when she gets halfway down. I laugh to myself. It can be hard to resist looking at the scene around you when you're flying through the air. I get distracted all the time when I'm in dragon mode. When she reaches the end and Brianna pulls her onto the platform, I jump and soar down to the platform myself much faster.

"There you are!" Ash thumps me on the back as I unhook myself. "Thought you guys fell or something."

"No, we're all good," I answer as I shoot another smile at Kristy. She smiles back at me, and I feel a little extra thump in my chest.

"Yeah," she answers. "We're all good here."

"Great," Ash says. "Can we go now?" He holds the next door open for us. With a nod to the girls, I'm the first to head on through.

11

Ash - Deciphering Spells… And Women

To be honest, the girls are pulling their weight way better than I expected. I actually am a little pissed with myself for questioning that so strongly as I did before we got into the maze. With Brianna, I had my doubts over the whole water magic deal and her dismal attitude towards me, which hasn't disappeared. And Kristy, she's a mortal. I thought the officials making the decisions had to have lost their minds to put a non-magical person in here. I even contemplated for a moment that she had done something to piss someone off, and this was their twisted way of removing the problem.

But no. Kristy has been brilliant this entire time. She sees things in a way none of the rest of us can. It's like her brain can absorb a puzzle in record time and flip it every which way in her head until it makes sense. And Brianna… she's still irritating, but she has skill. When we were up on the ropes course, she was moving so fast and with such ease. I tried to ask her where she had climbed before, but she was much more interested in racing away from me.

So I gave her what she was looking for. I chased after her, trying to best the same obstacles faster. We got tangled up together a bit in the cargo net, and her solution to the problem was to kick me in the shin! I doubled over, and she used that time to unhook herself from behind my hook to put herself in front, leaning her full weight into the net. When we both reached the end, she kept silent and stared off into the empty distance. I can't figure her out. She gets these bursts of agreeableness and then sinks back into a sullen state. She's getting on my nerves.

Kristy and Ash finally join us at the end of the course, and we make our way through the next door. To our disappointment, it's another freaking room. Is the Labyrinth going to keep going like this forever? No breaks, just endless chambers and challenges until we reach the end? This room is at least more interesting than all of the others visually. We stand in the middle of temple ruins with tall columns and a slowly crumbling roof. Each wall appears meticulously built piece by piece with gray and brown stone. Every few seconds, several pebbles tumble down from the ceiling and scatter across the ground. The floor is divided into large stone blocks carved with red glowing symbols. There are a few flickering torches along the walls that give us barely enough light to see.

I coax one of the flames down from the walls and spin it into a ball. This will allow us to see more of the room at once. I'm pleased to find that my magic is back and working well. I felt horrific when it was gone in one of the previous rooms. Felt way too vulnerable to be traipsing around a magical maze-trap. With a flick of my hand, I send the flames to float in the center of the group. Kristy shoots me a grateful look. I nod back to her before returning to inspect the pictures on the stones. Something about them seems very familiar, the cuts, the shapes, the non-descript edges. The answer's on the tip of my tongue.

Kristy is on to something as well. "Hey, can you bring the light a little closer?" She bends over to look at the stone in front of her. I flick the light to hover over her head. "These symbols here... I recognize them. If I could just remember..." She trails her fingers over the carving and presses down on one of the spirals.

Suddenly the stone drops straight down and practically disappears from existence. Kristy tumbles forward towards the abyss left by the hole and her arm slips down into the blackness. Kai throws his arm forward and grabs her leg before she can fall in completely. I join him by grabbing her other arm, and we drag her away from the hole. When she sits up, she breathes heavily and scoots back from the edge. She brings her legs up to her chest. Kai kneels next to her. "Hey. You good?"

She nods quickly. "I'm fine." Her voice comes out shaky at first before stabilizing. "I'm fine. She peers at the stones again around Kai's shoulder. "What the hell was that?"

"I'm not sure," I answer as I crouch down to study the ground again. "I guess there's certain stones we can't step on."

"I need to see them a bit closer," Kristy says as she crawls forward towards the edge again.

Brianna stops her with a hand on her shoulder. "Are you sure you want to get close again?"

"I have to," she counters. "I swear, I know these symbols." She studies them again. Then, like someone lit a fire under her, she leaps to her feet. Kai and Brianna have to grip her arms to stabilize her before she tumbles back where she started. "Ash. Ash, how familiar are you with elemental languages?"

Now that question throws me for a loop. I didn't think mortals had any interest in studying magical languages. They must look like gibberish to them. But when I take a look at the symbols again, I immediately see what she's going for. "You're right," I answer in awe. "You're freaking right, how the hell… how did you recognize that?"

"I had just started working on an independent study with Professor Arcada before the Labyrinth news was announced."

"What made you want to learn magical languages?"

To my surprise, she laughs lightly. "I love magic. I love the way it looks, the way it feels, and how unique each form can be based on the caster. If I can't cast it myself, I thought I might as well learn how to read the language that makes it possible for others. Thought it would help me study ancient history better in some of my other classes."

I chuckle and shake my head. Absolutely crazy. But also absolutely fucking brilliant. "Well, you're right." Kristy grins at that. "These symbols are a more archaic form of elemental language called Ebha. Most mages use a much more modern language now when learning spells, which is probably what you were starting out with. It's similar, but with more swirls and embellishments."

"How do you know that, Ash?" Kai asks.

I grin. "Hey, I do occasionally pay attention. But seriously, my father made me learn when I was a kid. I thought it was useless. It's been a while, but I still remember some things." I scan the stone floor for patterns. Then I spot two symbols on blocks that sit directly diagonal from each other only a large step away. "There!"

"What? What is it?" Kristy turns sharply and comes over to where I'm standing.

"See there?" I point. "Those two are the symbols for spark and light. Those are cause and effect spells. They go together."

Kristy doesn't hesitate in scanning the area around those stones. "There," she points to two wavelike symbols that swirl in opposite directions. "Is that... wave and ocean?"

"Wave and rain," I correct her. "The spell goes from rain to wave."

"That's old water magic," Brianna steps up behind me.

"Yeah," I respond shortly. "It's an old language."

"You recognize water magic spells too?" she asks.

I shrug. "Somewhat. It's all the same language. It's just a matter of which element you have an affinity for." Brianna is silent behind me, and I don't follow the subject further. "Someone needs to test those stones to see if they're stable."

"I'll do it," Brianna pipes up.

I turn around fast. "What?" I ask incredulously. "No. Kai should do it. He's got the flight magic."

"No. You saw how fast that stone fell when Kristy tapped it. I'm lightweight; if you hold on to me in case I fall, you can pull me away fast enough. It makes sense."

She's got a point. We don't know how quickly Kai will be able to activate his flight magic, and by then, it could be too late. "Alright," I concede. "Let's try." Brianna nods and moves up next to me. She offers me her arm, and I grasp it tightly. With a breath, she takes a big step forward onto the 'spark' symbol. The stone doesn't falter with one foot on, so she puts both feet on it. I keep a tight grasp on her one arm and lean over the stones to make sure she doesn't fall. Eventually, she gives me a sharp nod. "Let go."

"Are you sure?"

"Yeah." Carefully, I let go of her arm. We wait with bated breath. Luckily, there is no more movement. She hops back over to our safe stones. "I think we're good to go!" she cheers.

I grin back. "Alright, let's do it. Kristy, stay close behind me. We can interpret the other stones as we go along."

One by one, we make our way across the matching symbols. After the water spells, we find two more that indicate a breeze and a pair of dragon wings. Then a set of rock and tree symbols. The matching symbols repeat as we move across the floor. The whole task takes slow and careful movement, but we make it to the other side. When Kai steps off the last stable stone, the girls celebrate. Even Kai and I give a high five over their heads. It feels great when we make it through another obstacle. It's another step closer to the end and another step away from imminent doom. Part of me feels a little cheery.

Maybe we can get out of this.

12

Kristy - ESCAPE

The atmosphere is noticeably different as soon as we enter the next room. It doesn't measure up to the grandeur of the other chambers. Instead, we're in what resembles any old room in an old house no bigger than my living room at home. The only distinguishing feature is the ceilings that soar to a stunning height, at least a dozen feet. There's an odd collection of furniture and cabinets that don't seem to go together. Some are more modern while some are more vintage pieces. I swear the piano in the corner is from the 1800s. The room is certainly having an identity crisis: it's part living room, part kitchen, part storage area. When we file in through the door, it shrinks and disappears behind us. If the other doors hadn't also vanished once we stepped through them, I would have been concerned to be left in such a confusing space.

It isn't until a loud creaking from above our heads echoes through the room that I start to worry.

The noise brings all our eyes up to the ceiling. Scanning its perimeter, I can't spot anything that would have made such a sound. The walls meet the ceiling at all smooth edges, and the ceiling is just as blank. "Anyone see anything?" I ask absentmindedly as I spin slowly in a circle.

"No," Kai answers. "Should we be worried about that sound?"

Suddenly, a loud beeping noise to our right sounds off. We whip around to find a large red glowing timer with a twenty-minute countdown. Before I can process what that might mean, a message flashes harshly above it: ESCAPE. The countdown clock starts, and the loud creaking sound from over our heads restarts. This time, the ceiling physically drops six inches in one shot.

"What the hell?" Ash interjects.

"Oh no…" Brianna breathes nervously at the same time.

Immediately, I recognize what danger we are in. We're gonna be crushed if we don't escape in time. I don't hesitate in taking control of the room. "Okay," I start firmly. "Given the layout of the room and the timer, we're in an escape room. We need to look around for any and all clues, doesn't matter how big or small. Search for a place to start. Look in every drawer you can open. If you find a locked drawer, call out. That means there's probably a key hidden somewhere." A creaking from above echoes again, and the ceiling slides down a couple more inches, this time a little more smoothly. I glance up and gulp. "And try to ignore that for now. We got this."

All around me are fearful faces. We have been close to death several times since we started, but nothing like this. The dropping ceiling feels more purposeful and a hell of a lot more urgent. I don't want the others to get bogged down in their thoughts, so I make myself the first to jump into the search. I move to the closest cabinet and start pulling open the doors and checking every drawer. The others follow suit. The sounds above us are soon drowned out by the rapid opening and closing of cabinets.

"Make sure you're feeling around every corner and surface," I urge. "There could be hidden messages or keys stuck to the top of drawers that we can't see.

"Hey!" Brianna shouts.

I turn rapidly to find her with a glass of water in her hand. "What is it?"

"I found this glass inside of the fridge. It was the only thing in it. That has to mean something, right?"

I inspect the glass. "Possibly. I'm not seeing anything on the side." I tentatively reach my hand inside, and I collide with something smooth under my fingers midway down. "Wait!" The boys come over to stand with us as I pull a small clear ball out of the glass. "There we go!"

"Whoa," Brianna murmurs.

"Yeah," I chuckle.

"If we weren't fighting death, I would think that was cool," Ash offers as he plucks the ball out of my hands. Walking over to a circular wooden table, he throws it down, smashing it to pieces.

"What are you doing?!" Brianna shouts.

"No, no," I quickly reassure her. "That's a good instinct. An object like this usually has something inside." Sure enough, laying among the broken glass shards is a silver key. Kai carefully plucks it out and hands it to me. I shoot him a smile before asking, "Did anyone find a drawer that wouldn't open?"

"I found two in that chest," Ash points to a chest of drawers. "The second and third ones." I rush over and try both locks. The second one doesn't open, but the third one does. I open the drawer to find a small flashlight. When I pull it out and flip it on, a long purple beam shines towards the ground. I rush over to Kai and push it into his hand. "It's a blacklight flashlight. Look around the room; see if you can find anything."

"Why me?"

I blush lightly. "You're taller. Sometimes things are higher up on the wall."

Kai moves over to the walls and starts scanning. He is careful to move across the expanse slowly so as not to miss anything. As the ceiling starts to lower at a more even pace, Ash snaps at him, "Can you move any faster?"

"Don't!" I interrupt. "You don't want to miss something."

"I see something up here," Kai says as he beckons me over to another cabinet. I rush over and follow where the beam was cast. The light reveals a series of small drawings. A hand, a vulture, and a small pot with a triangle are all outlined in white. I recognize them from last year's class on ancient civilizations. I look over my shoulder at Brianna and Ash. "Ancient Egyptian hieroglyphs. The letters are d, a, and g."

"Dag?" Ash says, confused.

"Gad?" Brianna offers.

"The piano," Kai whispers.

I turn back to him. "What?"

"I wondered why there was a piano in here. It didn't really fit the style of the room. Those letters are all notes, right?" Before I can answer, he is already across the room, opening up the lid on the piano. To my surprise, his fingers brush across the keys right at middle C. It seems almost natural for him to place his hand there. He presses the notes on the piano in the order that I read them.

Two things happen simultaneously. Middle C pops off of the keyboard to reveal another small key, and the ceiling picks up speed in its descent. It soon reaches halfway down the walls. I wave for everyone to get on their knees. "Get down. I want to be ready for when that thing lowers further." Everyone complies. "Kai, over here." I wave for him to toss me the key. He throws it over, and I insert it into the third drawer.

I yank the drawer open to find a narrow-lipped flask with a key inside at the bottom. I try to reach my fingers inside to grab the key, but the opening is too small. When I try to pull the flask out to dump out the key, I find it fixed tightly to the bottom of the drawer. "I can't get this out!"

Kai rushes over to me and gives the flask a hard pull. It doesn't move an inch. "I don't know what to do," he panics, a rare tremor in his voice.

"We need to move it to the top. We could pull it out then," I theorize rapidly. "If we had gum and a string or something like that, I-" Like a lightning bolt, an idea strikes me. "Brianna, the water in the glass. The water." I'm stuttering, but she catches my drift. Ducking away from the low swinging chandelier which is now almost at head level, she whips her hand out and summons the water from the glass. She fires it over to us. The stream of water slips inside the flask and acts as a string, slipping itself inside the tiny hole at the top of the key and pulling it up. When it reaches the top, I pull the key out quickly with my fingertips. When I turn it over, I just catch the fading marker message of the word 'exit' and an arrow pointing down.

"Look around! On the ground! There's an exit-" I am interrupted by another loud screech followed by the grinding of gears. The ceiling begins to lower much faster, moving inches per second. It reaches the top of the furniture and continues to push down, slowly starting to crush each piece. Wood splinters and shards of glass begin to fly around us. The four of us move towards the center of the room, feeling around frantically for a groove on the floor while dodging broken pieces.

"Here!" Ash shouts as he runs his hand along the grouting between three tiles. "There's an indentation here." I throw the key to Ash who catches it one-handed. He shoves it into the dip in the floor, which crumbles away to reveal a key lock. When he clicks it open, he pushes down hard on the tiles. A section of the floor swings open into a black abyss. Without hesitation, he swings his feet over the edge and slides down into the hole. After a second, Brianna follows. Crawling over to the opening, I dodge several piano keys flying off the shattering piano before sliding in headfirst. The darkness overwhelms me, and I pray we come out into a much less dangerous chamber.

13

Brianna - Finally, A Reprieve

We made it out.

Well… not out, out. But we're out of the sequence of rooms.

When I hop down into the darkness in the escape room, I am free-falling the same way I did when the group first tumbled into the room with the mirrors. I brace myself, expecting to hit hard ground or be thrown into another restrictive trap. I even move my fingers into position so I can wriggle my way out of handcuffs or ropes if needed. But to my surprise, I land on soft, green grass. Two loud bumps indicate Kristy and Kai landing beside me. The blades tickle my cheek as I try to get my bearings.

When I sit up, I find myself in a wide circular clearing with Labyrinth ivy walls on all sides. There are a few interspersed trees to provide some shade from the bright sun. Ash crawls to lean against one of their trunks, breathing heavily after having the wind knocked out of him. Kai and Kristy shift around me and start to get to their feet. I decide to stay on the ground, rolling over and sitting up straight.

"Is this another room?" Ash looks around at the setting.

"I don't think so," Kristy shakes her head. "We appear to be outside again, but not like the fencing challenge or the high ropes course. Those areas had completely different appearances than what we saw at the beginning of the Labyrinth. This clearing looks more like the entrance to the maze, and the walls are back.

"Does that mean we're out?" I ask.

"For now," she answers. "I think we finished our first set of challenges."

A rush of temporary relief floods my body. I lay on my back and stare up at the sky. Finally. I take a slow, deep breath and soak up the sun for a moment. The heat feels good on my skin. It feels good to be out of there. I'm not someone who likes the fast-paced, constantly moving and shifting lifestyle. Back home, I had a plan. I had a routine. While things at school moved quickly around me, I knew how to keep my cool and keep going at a steady pace. I completed homework every day during study hall and sometimes after school before fencing lessons, and long-term studying was done in steady intervals throughout the week.

But here, I can't make a plan. The Labyrinth chooses our path. And for now, it chooses to allow us a break. And I am grateful for that.

When I sit up again, I find Kristy on her knees beside me, rummaging through the backpack she's been carrying since the first city. Oh, yeah. I look over to mine, which had tumbled off my back in the fall from the sky. We had been running around for so long and been so focused on conquering each challenge, I forgot I had it on. It became a familiar weight, I guess.

Kristy pulls two rolled-up sleeping bags and a tent out of her pack along with a few small hand tools. She motions for me to pass over my bag. I push it over to her, and she dumps it out to reveal the exact same items. Kai and Ash unpack theirs to find a reasonable supply of food in two small coolers, probably enough to last for three or four meals and cooking supplies. "The city didn't skimp on the supplies," Kristy muses. "This is good."

"Do you think it's going to be enough?" Ash asks. "Food is limited."

"The Labyrinth always provided for the city. I imagine it will provide for us too if needed."

"The maze couldn't provide a room?" Ash counters with a sarcastic chuckle.

"We should be grateful it gave us a place to rest at all," Kai interrupts. "Anyone know how to pitch a tent?"

"I do," I answer as I push myself up to a standing position.

"Me too," my best friend adds. The two of us each take a tent and start pitching them. Meanwhile, Ash and Kai break some branches off the surrounding trees to build the foundations of a strong fire. I appreciate them for building a platform for it instead of setting the grass on fire. Once our little camp is set up, we prepare a small meal for us of dried meat and cooked vegetables. We eat together but talk in pairs. Ash only speaks to Kai, and I only speak to Brianna.

When the sun goes down fully, the group turns in for the night. But I can't sleep. I'm too wired, waiting for something to happen. Would the Labyrinth snatch us away in the middle of the night? Could we wake up on the edge of a volcano or something? Could a creature come to attack us in the middle of the night? Why is everyone sleeping when so many things could happen? Looking over at Kristy, I slowly climb out of my sleeping bag and crawl to the tent entrance silently. When my friend doesn't stir, I leave the tent and head over to the remnants of our campfire to keep watch.

To my surprise, Ash is sitting on the ground, brooding and poking at the ashes with a stick. I freeze in place. *Why is he out here?* At first, I think maybe I should turn back and head inside. If he's awake and alert, there's no reason for me to be out here. No reason at all. But I can't head in and go back to sleep without a breath of fresh air to calm my nerves. Besides, Ash shifts his head sideways when I shuffle my feet forward and spots me. "Hey," he says shortly.

"Hey," I answer quietly. Swallowing audibly, I summon the courage to move over and sit on the ground across from him.

"What are you doing up?"

"I could ask you the same thing," I counter.

He gives me a quick chuckle. "Fair enough." He stares back down at the ground and begins poking idly at the ashes again. A sliver of unease creeps down my spine as he ignores me. I don't know whether to make conversation or just keep my mouth shut. But my curiosity gets the better of me.

"Why are you out here?"

Ash stops moving for a moment before answering, "Couldn't sleep. Thought I would keep watch."

"Me too. Didn't know if a challenge would start while we were asleep, so I wanted to be prepared."

"Same." Ash looks at me directly for the first time. His eyes are mild in color, but intense in their irritated expression. When he stares, I squirm a bit under his gaze.

"Why are you looking at me like that?"

"I don't really know what to make of you."

"What do you mean by that?"

Ash laughs harshly. "You've been hot and cold with me since we started this. I don't even know you. Like, who the hell do you think you are? What is your deal?"

I am taken aback by his attitude. Sure, I hadn't been the nicest around him, but I wasn't being a complete bitch. We were working together; we were getting through the day. What right does he have to be indignant? "I don't have to explain myself to you," I start.

"Bullshit," he interrupts me. "If we're going to work together and put up with each other all the time, I need to know if you're planning to leave me behind or let me fall to my death at the first sign of trouble."

"Hey!" I lean forward and raise my voice. "I don't know where you got such a low opinion of me, but I'm not the type to leave a fellow teammate behind."

"Then why the hell do you keep looking at me like I'm the scum of the earth?"

"You have a reputation! You were always getting in trouble. Everyone knows that. The parties, the drinking, the arrests. Come on, you must know that the entire school knew what you were up to at any given moment. I'm supposed to trust you with my life. Excuse me if I'm skeptical."

He scoffs. "So you're the type to believe everything you hear?"

"Of course not! I believe in what I can see. You parade around the school without a care, you act so much better than everyone else, getting caught up in every bout of trouble that comes your way. You were born with everything you could want, and you have used none of it."

Ash smirks broadly and leans back, cackling. "You think because I'm a rich kid and Daddy's the governor that everything was laid out for me?"

"You've been given so many chances, and you waste them."

In a fury, he jumps to his feet and gets in my face. He leans down until his forehead is mere centimeters from mine and I can feel his breath on my skin. "Don't think that just because you have some noble sense of morality that you know every fucking thing about the world. You know nothing about me. Keep your disapproving stares and your comments to your fucking self."

With that, he storms away towards his tent, and I am left reeling in his wake. I never would have guessed that he would react so strongly to hearing what people thought of him. I thought he always admired his reputation. Guess I was wrong. Part of me feels bad for having brought it up. The rest of me is just confused. I wait for almost an hour before heading back to sleep. I pick up the same stick that Ash had and draw small pictures in the dirt until my eyes start to drift shut. When I can't manage to sit up straight anymore, I return to my tent and wait for morning.

14

Brianna - Sirens and Seawater

I only manage to sleep for a few hours before a low sound wakes me from my light slumber. I sit up quickly, wiping the tiredness from my eyes and listening carefully. When the vibrations repeat, Kristy stirs beside me and opens her eyes. "What time is it?" she mumbles wearily.

"No idea," I murmur back. "But I think it's the Labyrinth."

"The Labyrinth?" Suddenly, Kristy is much more awake, pushing herself up to listen with me. This time when the sound comes, we both get to our feet and rush to the tent flaps to look for what danger lies ahead.

The outside has changed yet again, and this time, we find ourselves on a rocky shore, the two tents perched on the only patch of non-rocky sand. On our left is a tall blue and white lighthouse where a foghorn is sounding off from. The sun has been replaced by grey clouds and a light rain falls on our heads. In front of us lies an entire ocean going off into the horizon. Even my naiad senses aren't giving me a clear understanding of how vast the sea is. A long wooden floating dock stretches out several dozen feet over the water, and at the end floats a large anchored ship with billowing sails. The sea is choppy, but not enough to overturn the ship.

To my right, Kai and Ash emerge from their tent, both shirtless and disheveled. Upon seeing our location change, they immediately head back inside. Presumably to pack up, which is what Kristy and I should be doing as well. I motion to her, and the two of us maneuver our way around each other while crouched over to get dressed and pack up our sleeping bags. When everything inside the tent is in our backpacks, we venture outside to pack up the tent.

Kristy heads over to help the boys take down their tent while I collect the remaining items scattered around the beach. While our campfire is gone, the food and tools that we left outside still remain. I make a note to myself that we should probably keep that stuff close by in case the Labyrinth decides to snatch them next time. The four of us regroup on the edge of the sand before the rocks begin. "What's the plan?" I ask.

"Looks like we're headed to the ship," Ash answers as he swings one of the backpacks over his shoulder. I try not to look at him, instead keeping my eyes on the ocean in front of us. The naiad in me itches to dive into that water while the practical side of me contemplates how deep it might be or more importantly, how monster-filled it may be.

"We should be on our guard," I look over to Kristy instead. "Stay close to me, Kris. We have no idea what's in these waters."

"Aren't naiads supposed to have water sensing magic?" Ash asks me pointedly.

This time, I look up into his eyes. I don't want to think I'm not treating him the same as the others after last night's outburst. "I already tried doing a scan of the water, and I couldn't detect anything. I mean, I couldn't even figure out where this ocean stretches to. I wouldn't trust my senses at this point. Be prepared for anything."

Ash nods begrudgingly at me and begins gingerly climbing down the rocky hill, an uneven terrain that leads off the sand all the way down to the sea. The rest of us follow shortly behind. The rocks on the beach leading down to the dock are slick, sharp, and slippery. Kristy almost goes down twice. If Kai hadn't grabbed her arm and practically swept her off her feet onto a different rock, she would have fallen. When we reach the dock, Ash is the first to start walking across. The waves splash up on either side of us and occasionally spray us with seawater.

A few drops land on the back of my neck and send a chill running down my spine. I reach behind me to wipe off the water, but the chilling feeling remains. If anything, it intensifies. *Something's not right.* I stop and scan the water on either side of me. The waves are becoming a little choppier, and I can see something swimming underneath the docks. Multiple somethings.

"Hey guys," I say hesitantly. "Something's in the water."

Before my companions can answer, however, I hear soft melodic music echoing all around us. The tune has a mixture of violins and guitars and a soft flute floating over them all. I recognize the song, and it makes my heart run cold. Sirens. Before I can draw my next breath, four waves launch up on all sides of us, drenching the group in water. I cough as I am soaked and flip my hair back out of my face. In the wake of the splash, four beautiful women with long mermaid-like tails rise up to surround us. Each of them looks fairly similar with long dark hair and fair skin. Their eyes glow green like freshly cracked glowsticks and focus on us.

We're screwed.

"Whoa," I hear Kai exclaim.

"Get back," I call out. "Get back!"

Before anyone can move more than a step or two, the women open their mouths to add a haunting harmony to the music. They speak in an ancient language, the language of those who take and never give. In a moment, Kristy, Kai, and Ash freeze in place. Even I feel the icy grip of the sirens' power. Each line of their song pulls my teammates deeper under their spells. The magic does not affect me as strongly as it does them; I have a little siren blood in me on my mother's side. But I still feel the pull. I am not fully immune.

The siren sings to me of a more peaceful time, one where I was back at school with my friends. A world where I was popular and well-loved by everyone, top of my studies and top of the fencing tournaments. On the edge of my periphery, I see images of my family sitting around the table for family dinners. They're waiting for me. But I can't give in to the images creeping in.

The others are counting on me.

I run over to Kristy, trying to stop her from heading towards the edge. Falling in the water now would be certain death. They will all drown. Although she is moving slowly and so are the boys, it won't take long for them to reach the edge. I need to find a way to block out the sirens' song from their ears. I drop to my knees on the dock and wrestle my backpack off my back. I dump the contents out on the dock, searching for something that could help me, anything.

The solution hits me when I see my thin pajama top. I tear into the fabric ferociously, ripping it into several strips. Balling it up, I grip Kristy's arm before she steps off the edge of the dock and stuff the fabric into her ears forcefully. It doesn't block out all of the sounds, but it clearly blocks out enough because her glassy eyes blink back to normal. "Bri?" she questions tentatively.

"No time," I interrupt her and push another set of strips into her hands. "Get Kai." She immediately moves to him to pull him back from the edge.

Unfortunately, I'm a little too late for Ash. He takes a step and tumbles forward into the sea. The sirens all dive down after him. I don't waste any time in leaping in after him. I hit the water just in front of one of the sirens. She grins at me with slightly pointed teeth and lashes out at me with sharp nails. I narrowly escape her grasp and grab onto one of Ash's broad shoulders before he slips out of reach. Yanking him upwards, I kick towards the surface. As the sirens swoop in on us, hoping to drag us down to our doom, I send out an intense pulse of water magic through the sea. It sends them spiraling around us.

I break through to the surface, and Kristy and Kai quickly pull us out of the water. I shove the fabric into Ash's ears. The bewildered expression on his face when he snaps out of his trance haunts me. I leave him with the two of them and shove whatever I can from the dock back into my backpack. "Come on!" I shout. The four of us run towards the ship.

Rushing up the gangplank, I force the water to regurgitate the anchor from its depths. Gathering my strength, I will the waves to move us away from the dock and the dangerous creatures lurking around. We speed away towards the horizon.

15

Kristy, Kai, Ash - The Sirens' Song

Kristy

A crowd of people packs into the auditorium through the two sets of doors at the top of the house. A mix of students and parents dressed in semi-formal attire file in and mill about. No singular conversation can be made out; there is only a sense of excitement and anticipation in the sounds of their voices. When the lights flicker, they take their seats. The principal steps out from the curtains.

"Welcome to the graduation of the class of 2022," he speaks grandly into his microphone. The audience cheers. "Please welcome our seniors." The theater doors swing open, and my class strides into the room. They are met with thunderous clapping and shouting. A surge of pride races through my heart. We finally made it. Brianna is at my side. Kai and Ash follow, grinning brightly.

We take our seats in the front section of the theater, and the principal looks down at me. "Would our valedictorian, Kristy Fitzpatrick, please step up to the podium?" I rise and feel all eyes on me as I walk up to the stage. My parents and grandparents are chanting for me. "Kris-ty, Kris-ty, Kris-ty." I grin. I can't believe that my parents made it. That's all I've ever wanted, for them to show up on a day where I have this huge accomplishment to share with them. They watch me with proud eyes as I stride to the lectern. I step forward to speak. I open my mouth, and...

Suddenly, I am thrown from the stage and onto a wooden dock. Brianna, looking much more disheveled and without her graduation robe, presses both of her hands to either side of my head. I feel something soft in my ear. Cotton, perhaps. I look around me to find the waves in heavy turmoil and sirens... sirens swimming around, singing. The sound is muffled by whatever my friend has put in my ears. "Bri?" I ask her carefully.

"No time," she interrupts me and pushes a set of fabric strips into my hand. I recognize scraps of her pajama top. "Get Kai." At her words, I rush towards the man to stop him from tumbling over the edge.

Kai

I sit on the balcony of my family's beachfront property in Miami with my eyes on the beautiful sunset. The sky is lit up in a stunning pink that tapers off into orange and blue when it reaches the horizon. This is definitely the best place to sit in the entire house. You can watch all the action while being elevated above it all for the best view. I couldn't ask for a better evening.

Tonight, I decide which college I am heading to in the fall. The deadline is only a few days away, and I am still nowhere closer to a choice. I have three acceptance letters laid out in front of me. One is the whole nine yards: big school, athletic scholarship, the school that everyone at our school strives to get into. It's also the place where all my parents' work friends are major donors. It would be an easy way for them to move up in society around here. The second is a smaller school: strong academic programs with places to disappear with none of the pressure to perform. The last one is somewhere in the middle offering me an academic scholarship, a strong academic program, and a moderate amount of prestige. They're all great, really, but that one is probably my favorite.

My parents sit on either side of me, watching me excitedly. The anticipation is different than it usually is, however. There is little expectation there. "We want you to pick the school that is best for you," my father says insistently. "You've gotten into some fantastic schools, and we are so proud of you. Don't worry about our opinions or input."

"Go ahead, son," my mother encourages.

A rush of hope floods my chest. Are they really going to let me choose? If so... I know what I want. I look down at the letters again and open my mouth to announce my decision...

The sunset abruptly fractures around me and tumbles to the ground like glass. As I become aware of my surroundings, I feel something weird and smooth in both of my ears. Kristy looks up at me, moving her hands away from either side of my head. I reach up to touch two little balls of fabric in either ear. It is only then that I realize that there is chaos happening around me. Violent waves splash up on either side of the docks, four sirens sing and surround us, and my best friend steps off the dock and tumbles into the sea. Before I can react, Brianna comes flying across the platform and dives into the water.

"Come on!" Kristy shouts. "We have to help!"

Ash

I am finally flying free.

In the cockpit of a small plane, I tilt the aircraft to the right as I come in for a landing. It never gets old, the feeling of soaring through the air but being in control of every movement. I let the wheels come down from the bottom of the plane and slowly lead the vehicle into a smooth descent. When the wheels touch down, my body moves with that characteristic bounce of being back on earth. Except for the first time, I do not fear returning to the ground.

My uncle taught me to fly once I escaped from under my parents' grasp. He made sure I knew every procedure and safety guideline backwards and forwards before I applied for my pilot's license. Now I fly supplies and occasionally a small group of passengers up and down the Eastern Coast without a care in the world. And when the fun is over, my buddies and I head down to the beach to surf the afternoon away.

In the blink of an eye, I am in the water, paddling out on my board to catch the perfect wave. One grows before me: perfect size, perfect speed. I push myself up on the board to a standing position and move forward at just the right time to get up on it. Then...

Water.

Water filling my lungs.

I can't breathe.

When I open my eyes, I can't open them all the way. Water flows in. I'm surrounded by it, inside and out. A wistful melody rings in my ears so loudly; it's practically on top of me. I spin around, hoping to find some landmark to know which way to go. Smooth fingers with sharp nails scratch lightly at my clothes and my skin, brushing me over and over again. I attempt to fight it off by batting my hands. But it doesn't seem to be working very well.

Before I can orient myself, a solid pair of hands grips my shoulder and yank hard upwards. I fight it for a moment until the melody grows a little fainter and I realize the hands are pulling me towards the surface. I kick my feet as hard as I can to propel myself up. When my head breaks through the water, two different sets of hands pull me back onto the dock. The first thing I do is cough up what must be a gallon of water and wipe my eyes. But there's no time to process what just happened as two wads of fabric are shoved into my ears. I open my eyes widely to find Brianna staring at me, water sliding off of her in streams. *Did she dive in after me?*

She darts away from me as soon as I see her, collecting a variety of items that have been dumped across the dock and pushing them into her backpack. "Come on!" she shouts. Kai drags me to my feet, and the four of us take off running towards the ship.

Rushing up the gangplank and onto the ship, Brianna forces the water to launch the anchor from its depths. With a powerful manipulation of her hands, she wills the waves to move us away from the dock, leaving the sirens behind. We fly towards the horizon at top speed, and I hang onto the railing for dear life as we head for calmer waters.

16

Ash - The Ship

Once we are far enough away that the dock is a distant memory, I take stock of the vessel we have to work with. The ship resembles an old wooden pirate ship I remember seeing in a museum my father took me to. The main deck is large with two separate levels. We stand on the lower one now, amid trap doors under our feet and masts that lead up to billowing sails. The upper one sits above where I assume the captain's quarters must be, with the ship's wheel and a view off the back of the ship. A set of stairs leads up to the wheel while another set winds down into what I hope is a lower deck for sleeping. We need to do some exploring before we go any further.

"Hey," I signal to Brianna. Her eyes stay dead focused on the water ahead of us, hands shaking with the force of her water magic. Concerned, I move closer and raise my voice. "Hey." Her head shifts slightly sideways to indicate she has heard me. "You can stop now. We're far enough away from the docks and in calmer waters. Let's figure out where we need to go."

My words break through Brianna's haze, and she lets her magic slowly bring us to a floating stop. She stumbles when the spell finally breaks, and I grip her arm to stop her from falling. Her head snaps up to let our eyes meet. Her usual demeanor is gone; instead, exhaustion is practically radiating from her. Sweat drips down her brow, and her hands shake like an earthquake is happening only beneath her feet. Kristy comes over to ease her down into a seated position on the deck.

"You good, Brianna?" Kai walks over and asks.

"I'm fine," she breathes hoarsely. "I'm fine. Just give me a minute."

"Don't get up," Kristy insists. I silently agree with her.

"We need to figure out what we're supposed to do, where we're supposed to go," Brianna protests.

"We'll take it from here," I interrupt her. She looks at me with a puzzled expression, and I just say quietly to her, "Thank you." She seems to understand and sinks back to lean against the bottom of the railing. I wave for Kai to follow me, and the two of us step away to explore the ship while Kristy sits with her friend.

Thank you. It states so little. But what else am I supposed to say? I know I kinda went off on her yesterday, but she dove into a sea of sirens to pull my sorry ass out of danger. Most of me knows that she pretty much had to as my untimely death would have trapped the other three of them in the Labyrinth forever. But I'm not so sure she would have let me live if it wasn't for that. It's not that I'm not grateful. But I am confused.

Kai heads down into the lower decks while I enter the door on the main deck. As I suspected, I step through the door into the captain's quarters. The room is a good size with two beds against one wall and a bathroom around the corner. In the middle of the room sits a large map of the ocean with a few small landmarks indicated with small X's. I find a couple marked small landmasses as well as some sort of rocky cliff with a series of caves. Underneath the table holding the map, small ship figurines sit on two long shelves. Historically, these were often used to plan naval battle movements. I'm hoping that we won't have to make use of those. Not in the mood to fight another battle right now.

Behind the map table sits a mahogany desk and chair. A singular envelope sealed with a red stamp lays across the top, innocently holding the Labyrinth's desire to move us anywhere it chooses. I snatch the letter up and open the door back to the main deck. Kai has returned from searching below deck, and I wave him and the girls across the deck over to me. They enter the chamber.

Kristy looks around in awe. "This is so cool," she breathes.

"Yeah," I chuckle. "Pretty sweet, huh?" I turn to Kai. "Did you find anything down below?"

He nods. "Yeah, there's a kitchen down there that's fully stocked, a bedroom with two beds, and a modern bathroom. Not sure how that works, but it's there. It's somewhat of a cramped space overall, but the bedroom's a decent size. You can move around relatively easily."

"Good." I move over to the map and run my fingers over the docks marked on the map. "So we were just here. We're only a little ways north of that. The map doesn't indicate distance, unfortunately, but it does show direction."

"Where are we supposed to go?" Brianna asks. Her voice is starting to shift back to its normal volume and energy. I find it strange that I feel grateful for that.

I hold up the envelope and set it out on the table for the four of us to see. "I think the answer is in here. Who wants to open it?"

"I'll do it," Kristy pipes up and takes the message off the table. With careful fingers, she slits open the envelope and pulls out a single page.

"What does it say?" Brianna peers over her shoulder.

"It's handwritten," Kristy says with a hint of surprise. "It says in order to complete the next stage of the Labyrinth, we must travel by sea to the Caves of Mystere where there is a prisoner of the Labyrinth that we are supposed to free."

"Free a prisoner?" Brianna scoffs. "How? We can't even free ourselves."

"I guess the answer will become apparent when we get there." She turns to Kai and me. "Can either of you sail a ship? Brianna can't do the water magic thing the entire way." Brianna makes a sound in protest, but Kristy waves her off. "You know you can't. Don't argue."

"I can do it," I answer. Everyone turns to look at me.

"Didn't know you knew how to sail, man," Kai says.

I shrug. "My father loves boats. When I was a kid, my father insisted I learn how to sail. It's been a while, but I still remember everything."

"You and Kai should stay in here then," Kristy decides decisively. "If you teach him, you can navigate in shifts. You should probably teach us as well so we can join the rotation."

"Yeah, y'all can join in over the next couple days. I'm good to sail for now." I look down and refer to the map. "Looks like we need to head northeast. I'll set course right away."

"We'll get things sorted downstairs." Kristy smiles at me. "Good luck." Kristy and Brianna exit the quarters, and I move to the ship's wheel. After checking on the mainsails, I adjust the wheel to shift us east towards the rising sun. We catch a soft breeze, and we start to sail forward. I look out over the sea and wonder how far it extends and exactly how far we have to go to reach this prisoner. Here's hoping the journey takes long enough for me to figure out how to thank Brianna for what she did.

17

Kristy - Overcoming The Storm

Sailing across this mysterious ocean is calmer and quieter than any of the other challenges we have faced so far. It has been nearly forty-eight hours since we boarded the ship, and I haven't seen any signs of imminent danger. Of course, that puts me a bit more on edge, but it has been nice to have a little break.

Ash has been navigating us across the sea with some precise steering and adjusting of the sails. He stays outside for the majority of the day, moving back and forth between the upper deck and the captain's quarters to check the map. We can barely pull him away to eat something, let alone sleep. When he physically can't stay awake any longer, one of us remaining three takes over the night shift. Even then, he only lets himself sleep a few hours. It's strange, but I think he is trying to prove himself as useful to us. The incident with the sirens really seems to have shaken him up. He's certainly much quieter.

As for the rest of us, there's been plenty to do to help keep the ship running smoothly. We learn how to tie knots and rig the sails to keep us sailing in the right direction and take turns preparing light meals in the galley for each other. In the evenings, though, things are very slow. Brianna and Kai found a deck of cards hidden in a desk drawer in the captain's quarters and have been playing a ton of poker. I occasionally join in, but most of the time, I just listen to them play while I peruse the books I also pulled from the captain's room. They are mostly a selection of history books, a genre I enjoy, along with a few fiction pieces. Though if I read any quicker, I'll read through the whole ship before we're halfway to our destination.

This night feels a little different. The air is crackling with electricity, and a large mass of clouds is slowly creeping towards the ship. A steady gust of wind catches our sails and causes them to strain against their ropes. Ash calls us up from below deck to discuss the impending storm. "See that?" he gestures towards the sky. "That is a problem for us."

"How bad?" Kai asks.

"Pretty bad." Ash takes a hold of the wheel and shifts it just slightly to the right while keeping his eyes up at the sky. "When that storm hits, I am going to need everybody to stay up on deck. I'm gonna need a ton of help."

"Do we need to take the sails down?"

"No, we need to reef them." At my inquisitive look, Ash adds, "Lowering them partially and tying up the material on the booms there and there." He points to two beams a reasonable way up above our heads. I audibly gulp. Ash glances over at me before gesturing to Kai. "Can you take care of that?"

"Yeah," he answers before climbing up.

"Thanks," I mouth silently to Ash. If he saw me, I'm not quite sure because he turns to Brianna without a nod or a word.

"How much control can you have over an incoming storm?"

"Depends on how powerful the storm," she answers. "Based on the size of the clouds, I should be able to grant us a bit of relief."

"Good. Stand here." Gripping Brianna's shoulders with a distracted look in his eyes, he steers her to a spot by the rail at mid-deck. "Keep an eye on the storm. Any signs of change that you can sense, let me know.

When the storm hits, I want you closer to me by the wheel so I can hear you."

To my surprise, Brianna doesn't protest about being physically moved. I could have sworn she hated being forcibly taken anywhere. She only tightens her ponytail and says, "I can do that."

Ash finally turns to me. "Come with me." He walks me all the way to the front of the boat. A bright orange parachute-looking device leans against the side with a long line winding around a sturdy post. "If things get dicey, and they might, depending on the strength of this storm, I need you to toss this overboard and feed out this line until it opens, okay? It may keep us from taking a lot of damage. Can you do that?"

I test out lifting the piece. It's a bit unwieldy, but not so much that I can't handle it. "Yeah. I'll work it out."

"Great. I'm gonna stay at the wheel and try to steer us through this thing as best as I can. If you all listen for my calls of what to do, I think we'll make it through alright."

"Hey guys!" Brianna shouts from the lower section. "Incoming!"

When I look up to check on the storm again, I am aghast by how quickly it doubled in size. The clouds are much more menacing, and the wind starts to pick up dramatically. Ash's eyes narrow in concern, and he leaves my side to take control of the wheel. "This is gonna get ugly. Brianna!" he shouts down to her, "Whatever you can do, you need to do it now!"

I watch over his shoulder as Brianna grips the rail with one hand and readies herself magically with the other. I have never seen her cast such a large spell before. Her hand motions send swirling strands of air and water up into the storm clouds and bring larger strands of the same swirls down. The pieces form a tether between her and the sky, a pathway that she can attempt to control. As her magic takes hold, Kai rejoins us on the deck, jumping down the last few feet of the mast. He holds one of the ropes to steady himself. I grab onto the anchor's line myself. I've never spent this much time on a boat, let alone stand on a boat in the middle of a storm. I don't know what to expect. But if Ash's reaction is anything to go by, this is not going to be fun.

The storm glides over us, and all at once, the world is rocking. Waves that were once keeping us bobbing calmly are now crashing into us at full height and speed. Water splashes up along either side of the ship and adds to the rain plummeting down on top of us. I become blinded by the amount of foam hitting us from all sides. Strong gusts of wind threaten our reefed sails and even the masts near the top. In the brief seconds my view isn't blocked by water, I can see the more fragile sections near the top bending and straining with the force.

"Kristy!" I hear Ash's faint shout. "Drop the sea anchor now!" I immediately turn to drop the item overboard. The line begins to go in after it, and I grab it fast to feed it out to the desired length. It tugs at my skin, but I hold tight. When the anchor opens, I tie it off fast.

"*Can't you do any more with the storm, Brianna?*" Ash bellows at the top of his lungs.

Brianna whips around and growls at him. "If I could do more, I would be doing more! The storm is fighting my magic."

"What do you mean it's fighting your magic?"

"*Exactly what I said, you moron.*"

"Oh really?" Ash grunts as he struggles to keep the wheel from spinning freely. "I didn't see you calling me a moron when I was sailing us through the Labyrinth by myself."

"By yourself? We all pitched in! And what about Kai? He would take over for you more if you could tear yourself away long enough to let someone else help. At least he can admit to his own incompetence!"

"Hey," Kai snaps. "Don't bring me into this!"

"Bring you into this? Maybe if you would just reign in your boy better, people would stop bringing you into things involving him!" Brianna turns to yell at him.

"I am not his keeper! Why does everyone in the freaking world think I am his keeper?"

"I never asked you to be my keeper!" Ash shouts back.

Suddenly, the three of them are locked in an intense shouting match. Over what, I can't even tell. Ash's question was clearly out of irritation and worry for the storm and the intensity of the waves, and Brianna's response was out of her own frustration. I don't think I've ever seen Kai get angry before. Something doesn't feel right here. The waves grow steadily taller and continue to toss us around, more violently each time. Brianna and Kai are almost sliding from side to side on the deck as they argue. They keep shouting louder at each other over claps of thunder, which also seem to increase in volume as they do.

Wait... is that it? The storm is getting worse because they're fighting?

As my companions keep arguing, I take a moment to observe, hanging onto the side of the ship for dear life. The argument escalates, the storm gets crazier. With every insult, a clap of thunder. With every hurled phrase, a bigger wave batters the ship. There's no time to waste. If we want this to stop, they have to stop.

"Hey!" I try shouting, but my voice can't be heard above the sound of the storm. "Hey!" I scream louder. Kai, Brianna, and Ash ignore me. Or maybe they still don't hear me, I don't know. All I know is that a few more waves and the ship is going to break apart. We may go under. We can't drown here. We just can't.

In a rush of adrenaline, I know what I have to do. I have to get their attention. I let go of the chain I'm holding on to and curse to myself as I slide down the length of the deck to the center mast. As the boat sways dangerously, I stare up at the cross beam where I could feasibly hold onto. *This is by far the dumbest idea I have ever had.* Gritting my teeth, I begin to climb.

The height mixed with the swaying is terrifying. My heart is pounding in my chest. I don't know what I'm doing. All I can do is put hand over hand, one foot in front of the other. When I reach the crossbeam, I wrap my arms around it and hoist myself up. "Hey!" None of them see me at first. *"Hey!"* I shout.

Finally, Kai glances up as if annoyed by my noise. His eyes widen, and he breaks out of his angry trance. "Kristy? What the hell?"

Brianna is next to look up. "Kris! Get down from there!"

I look down as the ship sways vigorously again and feel my stomach rise in my throat. "I would if I could!"

"What are you doing?" Ash yells up to me.

"Your arguing! It's fueling the storm. You have to…" My head sways dizzily as another gust of wind blows against me. "You have to stop."

"Hold on, Kristy, I'm coming to get you," Kai tells me frantically as he begins to climb up after me. He reaches me in record time and helps guide me down to the deck. As we make our way down, the storm begins to fade almost as quickly as it began. By the time both my feet are on the floor, the storm is gone.

18

Kai - There's Something About Her

As the storm finally subsides, the state of the group feels uncertain. When I help Kristy down to the deck, everyone stands around staring at each other. Although our fight was magic-driven, there were things said that revealed tension in places I didn't even know there was tension. I mean, Brianna and Ash have been at each other's throats pretty much the whole time, so their argument over petty stuff is normal enough. But my part in all this? My statements? It's like they came out of nowhere and ripped themselves from my chest.

I never thought that I was Ash's keeper before, like he was someone I was supposed to keep track of. Or maybe I had. We have been friends for a long time, way before Ash started getting into trouble. I remember meeting him when we were in the first grade and chasing each other around on the playground. It used to be so easy. It's still easy, right? But I can't deny to myself that sometimes I feel overwhelmed trying to keep him from completely screwing up his life.

Ash looked at me with an unreadable expression as he handed off the wheel to me for the night. I would have pushed, but I've been friends with him long enough to know that sometimes he needs some time alone to not explode. Hopefully he doesn't explode. His anger and stress come out in uncontrollable bursts of fire, and I'm not looking to be burned tonight. Maybe I should take the whole night shift and not switch off with Kristy. That may be safer.

I keep my hands on the wheel, making small slight adjustments as I gaze out over the calm sea. It's so dark out now. The ocean looks nearly black, only lit up by the full moon looming above. Now that the clouds have cleared, the sky shows the tiniest twinkling stars. It's exactly like what you would imagine when you think of that eerie quiet after a big storm. I take a minute to close my eyes, resting my forehead against the wheel and trying to reset my brain.

"Kai?" A soft voice speaks in front of me.

My eyes fly open to find Kristy standing in front of the wheel. She's dressed in a T-shirt and a pair of loose pants, pajamas I'm assuming. Her hair hangs loosely on top of her head in a ponytail. She gives me a soft smile as she angles her head up slightly towards me.

"Hey," I reply in light surprise. "What are you doing up here?"

She shrugs and turns to look over the railing. "I couldn't sleep. Every time I close my eyes, I feel the swaying of the ship from when I was up so high. I don't like it very much." She absentmindedly rubs her hand against her arm, her eyes cast down to the deck.

"Oh." I don't know what else to say besides that, so I reach over and pat her shoulder awkwardly. "I'm sorry."

She throws me another half-smile over her shoulder. "Don't worry about it. Thought a breath of fresh air might cure me."

"Well, you're welcome to stay up here as long as you want."

"Thanks." Both of us look out over the water in silence for a while. I notice the way the wind blows through her ponytail, rustling the edges. Her hair is really delicate. It's strange to me to look at the way she talks when all of this super-smart jargon is tumbling out of her mouth, but other times, she seems fragile. I'm not sure what to do with that.

"Hey, can I ask you something?" Kristy interrupts my nervousness.

"Yeah, sure. Whatever you want."

"Did you mean what you said about Ash?"

Ah. That. The one question I didn't want to answer. I laugh shortly and rub the back of my neck. Kristy cringes sheepishly. "Oof, I'm sorry. I wasn't supposed to ask that, right? Please ignore me. I didn't think before I spoke. Please get it."

"No, no," I quietly reassure her. "Don't apologize. I just don't have a good answer."

"What do you mean?"

"Well, of course Ash and I are cool. We wouldn't hang out if we weren't. I just... it can be hard to be in charge all the time, you know?"

"Yeah." She chuckles. "I know what you mean."

"You feel like you're in charge?"

"A lot of the time. I'm supposed to be the smart one. Know all the answers, be the straight A student, be okay by myself all the time. It's hard."

"Yeah," I nod with her. *She does get it.* "I just want to choose my own path, you know."

"Do you feel like you can't?" Kristy fully turns to me and puts her back up against the railing.

I shrug. "Sometimes. It's complicated."

"Try me."

I raise an eyebrow but decide to press on. "Well... I'm an athlete. I'm probably going to get my pick of athletic scholarships. Likely at big schools with a certain kind of reputation, you know. Large donor schools. My parents have always wanted me to go to one of those, make them look good and bring them into the right social circles. They seem to think that places like that would be a big opportunity for me to emerge, I guess."

"And you disagree?"

"I mean, I guess so. Those schools are just not... something I imagined for myself, I think."

Kristy moves closer to me and peers over the top of the wheel again. "Well, what do you imagine for yourself?"

"What do you mean?" I lean forward a bit and rest my forearms in between the spokes of the wheel.

Kristy chuckles softly as her face flushes a slight pink. "I mean, what does your ideal path look like?"

I tilt my head as I think over the question. No one has ever asked me point blank before. Even the guidance counselor came with preconceived notions about what I wanted out of college and life. So I never really thought about forming a complete plan because no one ever cared enough to ask. "I'd like..." I stop. "I don't fully know what I want," I admit.

"That's okay. Me neither. Just... say something you want."

After a moment, I answer, "I'd like to work for a nonprofit. Either the service side or the business side. Maybe both."

"That's great!"

I grin. "You think so? Yeah, I've always enjoyed working in student government and all the service initiatives we fund and fundraise for. I think I would like to do that as a job."

"You would be great at it." Kristy beams at me, and I can't help but silently admire her.

"What do you want to do, Kristy? What's your path?"

She glances down and shuffles her feet. "I'd like to be a teacher. In what subject, I'm not quite sure. History, ancient languages, English, maybe."

"You'd be a good teacher."

"Thanks."

"Why teaching?"

"Oh," she breathes, "I'm just really good at academic stuff. I love chasing after a strand of research and following the trail as far as it goes.

I like finding connections and learning how those connections tell us something about the world or an author. I want to teach other people to love those things too. Maybe a college professor."

I smile at her. "That's cool."

"Yeah…" Her voice trails off as she tips her head all the way back to see the sky. "Beautiful stars tonight."

"Yeah…" I breathe. "Beautiful." As I watch Kristy enjoy the sky, I feel like I'm seeing her for the first time. And I think… I think I might like to keep seeing her.

19

Kai - Finding the Cave

The night spins past in me in a tiring haze of staring into the same dark scenery for hours. Kristy stays with me for a while, talking idly until I send her back to bed when she can barely keep her eyes open. I must have fallen asleep at the wheel standing up at some point because when I open my eyes, the sun has risen in the east. The light casts a strange orange glow on the water. When I collect my bearings, I look out into the ocean and stumble back at what I find. "Hey!" I shout across the ship. "*Hey!* Everybody get up here! Come on!"

Ash comes stumbling out of the captain's quarters, looking like he's been abruptly awoken from a deep sleep. "Dude, what the hell?" When he looks out to where I am pointing, he almost immediately snaps out of his state. "Whoa."

Kristy and Brianna come running up from below deck and rush to the railing. Kristy lets out a loud whoop. "There it is!" she cries. Jutting up towards the sky, a large rocky cliff floats in the distance. If I squint, I can just make out the mouth of a cave beckoning us to enter.

"There it is," I breathe. My chest fills with a rush of pride every time we manage to reach the next stage of a challenge. Every movement, every choice brings us one step closer to getting out of here. But I have to admit, I am kind of enjoying the adventure and chaos of it all. I never do anything this exciting and unexpected at home. Even soccer has somewhat of a limited set of outcomes. This... this is unlimited possibility. For the first time in my life, there are no limits.

"Well, what are we standing around for?" Ash asks with a laugh in his voice. "Move." I step out of the way as Ash takes the wheel. "Adjust the sails." The rest of us move to unfurl the sails and shift them to catch the wind. We speed towards the rocky mountain with hearts high. Kristy smiles brilliantly as she hangs onto the railing, getting sprayed by the surf. I go up to join her. We gaze out over the water as the island grows closer and closer.

When we reach the rocky cliff, Brianna drops the anchor overboard to steady us. The water is deep enough, surprisingly, that we are able to drop anchor fairly close to the rocks. "How are we gonna reach shore?" She looks around the deck for answers. "I didn't see any kind of lifeboat on board."

"The gangplank?" Ash offers.

"Is it long enough?"

"We should find out." Ash walks over to engage the gangplank. With a couple of extra planks found below deck, we are able to reach across to a stable point on the cliff. I take the first few steps across to check for stability before quickly making my way to the other side. I hold down the other end of the boards while my three friends make their way across. I gather a few heavy rocks to hold the plank down while we make our way up to the cave. Of course, they won't hold at all if a storm or a strong gust of wind blows in. But it's gonna have to do for now. I imagine the Labyrinth wouldn't trap us on the island unless we were supposed to be.

In theory.

We don't even need to discuss a plan for this anymore. It only takes a glance before we are moving as one to the pathway that spirals up to the cave. We work fluidly together, hiking up the rock face, grabbing each other's arms and sometimes legs to keep each other from slipping. Kristy has the most trouble, or at least the slippiest shoes, as she describes. I catch a limb almost every thirty seconds. When we reach the cave's opening, Ash and I exchange glances before taking the lead.

"Move slowly!" Kristy interjects. "We don't know what kind of traps we might trigger."

The mouth of the cave looms large over our heads as we step inside. It is only then that I see the structure is less like a cave and more like a series of tunnels that twist and lead every which way. We have no choice but to rely on pure gut instinct and make our way down the tunnel to our left. I only hope it leads to wherever the prisoner is being kept.

A ways in, Brianna suddenly cries out. "Stop!" When Ash takes another step anyway, she throws out her hand and yanks him back just as a massive pendulum blade swings out from the ceiling down to narrowly miss the side of his head. "Dude, you have to stop doing that."

Ash breathes heavily and bats her hand away in frustration. "Okay! Okay." He may seem irritated, but I can tell he's a little shaken up.

Kristy picks up a rock and tosses it a few feet in front of us into the dirt. As soon as it lands, the blade engages again, swinging across a certain field. "The bottom of the blade is a couple feet from the ground." To my surprise, she lays flat on her stomach on the ground. "We should be able to pass through by belly-crawling like this."

I grip her ankle before she can start. "Are you sure?"

She gives me a little smile over her shoulder. "Yeah."

I nod and lay down on the ground beside her. By reaching our hands in front of us, we pull ourselves across the dirt inch by inch. The blade drops low above us, but as Kristy predicted, it slides right above us without even touching the back of my shirt. Brianna follows us as does

Ash, after a little hesitation.

I pull Kristy to her feet, and we move forward deeper into the cave. The choices of which way to go begin to increase now. Each fork now has three or four various entrances to choose from. There are no markings on the walls, no differences, nothing that might guide us further. I suggest that we take turns choosing which direction to go, and everyone goes along with it. I find it almost comical that we've resigned ourselves to having no clue.

Finally, we spot a light at the end of the final series of tunnels. We rush forward where the cave begins to open up to find a chamber surrounded by stalagmites and stalactites. There are so many points jutting out of the ground and down from the ceiling that we are forced to stop in our tracks and carefully maneuver our way around the spikes. At every turn, we're likely to get stabbed.

"Where's the prisoner?" Ash asks me in a hushed voice.

"No idea."

"Hello?" A male voice calls out from the interior of the maze of spikes.

The four of us freeze. Kristy shouts back, "Hello?"

"In here!"

In there? It's an absolute mess of spikes and twists that are impossible to see through. "Can anybody fit?" I ask.

"We all should be able to if we're careful," Brianna answers. She is the first to ease her way through the first set of spikes. She moves gingerly around the obstacles. Kristy follows right after. Thank goodness we all have some sort of athletic ability because this would be almost impossible without it. We all make our way through the maze of spikes until we reach an open pocket in the center. Once inside, we find a middle-aged gentleman with brown curly hair with a touch of gray in it. He raises his head to look me dead in the eye.

"*Finally.* I've waited ages for another set."

20

Ash - Protecting Her

I can't believe there's actually someone in here.

I mean, I know that the Labyrinth usually has some kind of purpose for sending us in the direction it does. The reason doesn't always seem apparent in the moment, but eventually, a pathway opens up. But the rules continue to be unclear. Is this guy a challenger who got caught here? Is he a random man who tried exploring the Labyrinth and paid the price?

The prisoner in the center of the cave sits rigidly in a stone chair. He looks like he's been here a while, but not terribly long as there's still a little bit of youth to him. He's got facial hair all along the sides of his face and around the base of his neck. When he looks up at us, his eyes sparkle, a mixture of mad delight and desperation. I narrow my eyes at this. We need to keep on our guard. Who knows whether freeing him is the best decision.

Though it is the directive. Dammit.

"Tell me, how long has it been?" the man asks.

"How long?" Kristy questions. "What do you mean?"

"What year is it?"

"2021. Why?"

The man sighs deeply and lets his head fall down into his hands. "It's been two hundred and eighty-nine years," he mourns to himself. I recognize the pain in his voice. It's the way my voice sounds when I'm alone and talking to myself in the mirror after a fight with my parents. That sound of being resigned to being trapped for the foreseeable future. Imagine being imprisoned alone for that long.

"Have you been here the whole time?" My voice sounds rough coming out of my throat. The others turn to look at me.

The man raises his eyes to stare at me and shakes his head lightly. "Not the whole time. But most of it. I have been freed ninety-seven times over the last three centuries. The Labyrinth sends me to the next closest city of challengers, and I wait there until someone fails. Then I find myself back here in this chair where I started to wait for another group to move through."

"The magic sends you back?" Brianna is horrified.

"Yes. All the way back."

Kristy gulps. "Well, let's get you out of here. Can you tell us anything about what kind of enchantments are needed to free you?"

The man sits forward in his chair. "Please tell me one of you has water magic."

Brianna steps closer to him. "I'm a naiad."

The man smiles. "I am a naiad as well. What's your name?"

"Brianna."

"I am Nelius. You're the only one who can free me."

"Just me?"

"Just you." He gestures to four specific spikes at four corners around him, aimed at the legs of his chair. "Those four cast a field of fire any time anyone tries to move past them. The intensity of the flames only increases depending on what kind of creature is passing through the field. But it takes a certain amount of heat to trigger the system to shut itself off entirely and allow me to escape. The highest heat level needed to free me can only be achieved by someone with water magic. A cruel paradox, for the element least likely to aid in growing a fire to be the only way that the fire can grow enough to free me."

"Will the fire burn me?" Brianna asks.

"Likely. Most who try end up with a burn of some kind. But it is the only way to go forward."

I watch Brianna's face slowly crumble from a steady determination to a quietly building fear. I can see in her eyes that she is still going to tackle the task, but she doesn't feel right about it. She gulps before giving a single swift nod. "I can do it," she says.

"Wait." Kristy grabs onto Brianna's arm to stop her from moving forward. "You can't walk into this without a plan. You could get seriously hurt, Bri."

"We don't have a choice, Kristy," her friend argues back. "It's not like we can avoid the issue."

"She's right, you know," Nelius chimes in. "You need to free me to move on to your next set of tasks."

"Well, I'm sorry, but if everyone sent their water mage or naiad into the flames to save you without a plan, it's no wonder you end up back here every time," Kristy snaps. The prisoner has the sense to look slightly apologetic under the intensity of Kristy's glare. I resist the urge to smirk. The girl then turns to Kai and me. "What can we do?"

"Don't look at me," I reply. "I have no idea."

"How can we test to see how strong the flames would be? How fast do they trigger the system?" Kai asks. He always comes up with the right questions.

"I could stick my arm quickly past the field to see," Brianna suggests.

"No, Brianna, let's—"

"Kristy. It's the best way. You know that."

Kristy grumbles, but lets go of Brianna's arm. "Be careful."

Brianna walks over to the boundary between us and the naiad

prisoner. She cautiously reaches out a hand before thrusting it towards Nelius. Immediately, each of the four spikes at the corners of the man's chair shoots out a red-hot stream of flames. Those flames combine together to generate intense walls of fire surrounding the chair trapping the prisoner. Brianna yanks her hand back fast before she can be singed by the flames. Her eyes flick over to mine, and for a moment, I catch a glimpse of true horror on her face.

She's terrified.

"No," Kristy states simply. "No. You're not doing that."

"I have to," Brianna answers, her voice shaky.

"I'm not letting you do that!"

"Kristy!" she shouts. "Shut up already! Stop telling me that I can't do that or I don't have to do that because you're just plain wrong. You're not helping." Kristy's mouth tightens, but she doesn't say anything else. Brianna turns back to Nelius who gives her a solemn nod and holds out his hand to the edge of the barrier. She moves to try again.

"Stop." I say quietly.

She pauses and glances over her shoulder at me. "Why?"

"Because I may have an idea." I walk close to her. "Have you ever put up a shield before?"

"A couple times. But the water would evaporate right away from the heat."

"I'm not suggesting a water shield. A fire one."

"Um…" She raises an eyebrow. "In case you haven't noticed, I don't have fire magic."

"I am aware of that," I snap at her in exasperation. *Why won't she just shut up and let me finish explaining before shooting my idea down?* "I meant, let me try putting a shield around you."

"That could work," Kai thinks out loud. "If you can hold the shield long enough, the flames will merge with the shield and make the shield stronger."

"Or they could attack the shield," Kristy counters. "Do you think you can withstand it if they do and keep the shield up?"

I turn to Brianna. "To be honest with you, I have never held a shield over someone else before. I know how, but I've never put it into practice. But my personal shields are strong enough to withstand a lot. Will you let me try?"

Her eyes bore into mine as she contemplates my offer. *Come on, Brianna. Just trust me. Just this once. We can go back to hating each other in a minute.* Finally, she sighs. "Alright. Let's give it a go."

When I raise my hands to put the shield up, she visibly flinches. My breath comes out in a rush. *She thinks I'm gonna hurt her.* "Look," I speak to her in a low voice. "I'm going to try the shield. It's not gonna burn you. I promise."

"You promise?" Brianna lets out a soft wry chuckle. "I thought you hadn't done this before."

I softly chuckle and nod to her. "Fair enough. Then I swear I'll try my best. Can you accept that?"

She grants me a small smile. "Okay." She closes her eyes. "Go ahead."

I lift my hands again and concentrate on the outline of her body. I try not to examine too closely how much I'm noticing how many ways it curves. Pushing forward, I let the flames flow from my fingertips and surround her gently. With a little more effort, I am able to expand the field until the shield completely envelops her. When she opens her eyes, they widen at how close the flames are to her. But when she doesn't feel any pain, she grins at me.

It's brilliant, really. And the first time I've seen her smile directed at me.

Kinda nice for a change.

I motion for her to try again. This time, when she reaches out her hand to take Nelius's, the flames collide with my shield. Kristy wasn't wrong; it's a hell of a lot more effort to keep the shield from collapsing.

They are pressing against my magic with a lot of force like trying to keep a truck from steamrolling over you. Luckily, Brianna doesn't waste time yanking Nelius out of the fire field. They both hit the ground, and I let the shield drop. I don't realize how much energy the spell took out of me until my knees hit the dirt and my vision blurs.

Kai rushes over and yanks me to my feet, supporting me on my right side. "You did it, man."

When I blink away the exhaustion, I find Brianna in front of me, looking concerned. "Are you alright?" Her eyes search mine for answers.

"Are you?"

"I'm fine," she answers while shaking her head. "You did it."

"Told you I could." My laugh feels painful in my chest.

All around us, the spikes from the ceiling and walls are slowly receding into nothingness. A pathway opens up to the outside, and I can hear the ocean calling us back to the ship. With my arm over Kai's shoulder, we walk towards the sunlight.

Another challenge gone.

21

Brianna - One More Try

Our little group boards the ship with Nelius in tow and pulls away from the rocky shore. The table in the captain's quarters shows us a new map with a clear pathway to a new branch of the labyrinth. With a recovering Ash by his side, Kai sails us towards shore. Kristy and I stand at the front of the ship with Nelius to learn more about his time trapped in the Labyrinth and what we might be able to expect from the maze next. I can't help but keep glancing back over my shoulder at Ash.

I wasn't expecting Ash to step up and find the solution to getting me through the final challenge. When his shield came up around me, I was frozen in fear, half expecting his magic to consume me. But he managed to keep the flames from touching me. There was such concentration on his face. Honestly, I've never seen more effort from him than at that moment. And I have been watching.

That's the thing. Really only Kristy knows this, but I have been watching Ash. He was always the arrogant type. I didn't just say it because of his attitude. I watched his actions. Since we started high school, he's always been the first to crack a joke in class rather than answer the question that's been asked. In between classes, he would often stride down the hall with no care in the world where he was going or who he crashed into. He was late all the time. Four out of my six classes were with him. I know what I'm talking about. But somewhere underneath all of that, he might have a brain. And a conscience, apparently. I'm still skeptical, but… he did assist me. I suppose I should thank him more directly. I'll have to when we stop.

We reach shore only a couple of hours later. When we dock the boat, collect our belongings, and disembark, the boat shimmers and vanishes like it never existed. Can't say I'm surprised, but the various vanishings do give a sense of finality to each stage of the Labyrinth. Nelius gestures to the group. "Follow me. I'll take you to your resting spot."

"Where are we now?" I ask.

"A little town dubbed Iron Point. The founders named it after the spikes in the caves on the island. Many of them failed there, so it seemed like a fitting name." He leads us up the sand dunes on the beach to a long wooden boardwalk. We walk up a small ramp to reach a pathway that stretches out all along the length of the beach. He leads us north for a ways past some gazebos and alternate entrances to the shore. Eventually, he points us towards a small beach house at the end of one of the branches. "The little house is yours."

"Thank you," Kristy responds. Kai and Ash begin separating from the group, headed towards our resting spot.

"Wait!" Nelius suddenly calls out. The four of us freeze in place, staggered across the boardwalk. "There's something important I need to tell you about the Labyrinth."

My eyes widen. *Are we about to get an answer about the inner workings of the maze?* "What is it?" I ask.

"I was put here because I wronged its creator."

"There's a creator?" Kristy blurts out. "What do you mean there's a creator?"

"You're telling us someone actually theorized and built the Labyrinth?" Ash whistles.

"That's ridiculous," Kai chimes in. "No one has ever found any evidence of any singular person behind the maze."

"None that made it out to the public. Over time, I have spoken to many challengers, many, many people who failed. Many of them failed because they relied too much on what they saw as the rules of the maze. Follow the instructions, but don't search for patterns. The first time you look for a correlation between one challenge and another, you will fail. You were taught that the magic here is unpredictable. It's more than that. The magic is predatory. Every aid the Labyrinth gives you is another element for it to take away if you piss the Labyrinth off. Do not fight it. Go with the flow. Don't get too cocky."

His voice is quiet, but his eyes are dead serious. *Don't mess with the maze. Don't get comfortable.* That's a horrifying thought, especially as we are about to go rest in a place the Labyrinth provided. If we relax too much, we'll fail, but if we don't relax enough, we're going to drive ourselves crazy. Part of me is angry that this was the important piece of information he needed to tell us. Not only are we nowhere close to understanding this maze, now we're gonna be paranoid too.

"Thank you, Nelius," Kristy responds after a while, ever the polite soul. I keep my mouth shut. Cause if I say something, it won't be as friendly.

Nelius simply nods in acknowledgment. "Good luck, all of you. Safe travels." With that, he turns around and walks down towards the opposite end of the boardwalk.

The four of us stand in silence for a minute or so before Kai breaks us out of our trance by starting off towards the house. When we reach the property, we go inside to find a one-room home with a small kitchen, bathroom, and two queen-size pull-out couches. Guess we're sharing beds tonight. It's kinda weird for the Labyrinth to put us all in one space when we have been separated thus far. But I'm trying not to worry too much about that. My focus is on speaking to Ash.

Once I put my stuff down and understand the lay of the house, I turn around to pull Ash aside. But he has disappeared. I spot him out the window down on the little private beach by the water. With a pat on Kristy's shoulder, I exit the house and leave her and Kai to their own devices. I approach Ash quietly. I'm kinda afraid that if I startle him, he may not speak to me.

If he notices I'm behind him, he's not acknowledging it. Instead, he stares out at the water intently. His eyes barely blink as they scan the horizon. I clear my throat. "Hey." He doesn't respond. I continue anyway, "Thank you for what you did back there. The shield… it was really impressive."

"You're welcome," he answers gruffly.

"Really… I could have been badly burned, and the shield worked. So… thank you."

He lets out a short huffing laugh. "You don't have to thank me again."

"But-"

"Hey." Ash finally turns around to look at me. "I did what I needed to do. You saved my life with the sirens. I thought I at least owed you one. But that doesn't mean we're friends. I paid a debt. That's all it needs to be."

I resist the urge to sigh loudly. *Here we go again.* "Nobody's asking you to be friends, Ash. I was trying to say you had a smart idea, that's all."

"Of course it was. I do occasionally have a coherent thought."

This time, I do sigh. "Why do you have to be so hostile?"

To my surprise, he shakes his head, and his lips quirk up. "Look, hostility is what I know. It's who I am. And it's not like you and I get along very well to begin with. I don't know how to talk to you. What am I supposed to say? Can't we just call it even… call it a day? This shit is complicated enough without throwing conversation in the mix."

"Don't you ever get lonely?" I ask. "Does it not get tiring not talking to people, not asking questions, just being by yourself?"

"I got Kai. That's enough for me. If you've got one good friend, do you really need more? Do you not feel that way about Kristy?"

"Kristy's my best friend, but she's not my only friend. I like to have a variety of people to hang out with, to talk to. To have fun."

"Are you looking to add me to your list?"

The question causes me to stutter. "N... No, not-"

"Then let me be." He turns back to the shoreline. "Don't ask for more from me. I'll be useful, I'll be helpful, but I won't be friendly. Don't ask me to be."

"But why?"

"That's my business. Now please go. I need time to think."

I want to say something else, but his tight lips make the words falter on my tongue. With so many more questions to ask, I turn around and head back to the house. There's nothing more for me to do.

Continue The Story!

The Ivy Labyrinth: Volume 2 —> Releasing in Winter 2022/23

If you just can't wait to read more, check out The Ivy Labyrinth on Kindle Vella and Radish!

Acknowledgments

I want to take a moment to thank the people who have helped bring my serial fiction story and later, this first volume, into existence. First and foremost, I would like to thank my beta readers, Jennifer Roachford and Morgan Hammer, for helping me to keep my story on track. Next, my amazing cover designer, Milan Krstevski who signed on to yet another one of my projects and pulled off a fantastic cover. I would also like to thank my amazing group of readers for continuing to be supportive of this story as it continues to unfold. You all are my favorite part of the process. Finally, I want to thank my family and my boyfriend, Daniel for their support during my entire publishing journey. I love you all.

About the Author

Cady Hammer has been a writer for most of her life. From the time she was eleven years old writing her first novel between classes, she always looked to the world to bring inspiration. She was often teased for being in her own world, but never hesitated to invite others along on the adventure. She now spends her time at the College of William and Mary pursuing a Bachelor of Arts in History and minoring in Anthropology.

Cady is the author of the Chasing Fae trilogy and loves to create stories that take people away from the world for a while. She creates her universes with inspiration from her studies, trying to create a place that feels so real that readers have to explore it. These stories explore the complexities of relationships crafted around the idea that love, friendship, and grief are all interwoven. She hopes to one day become a bestselling author alongside her desired career in museum work.

You can connect with me on:

🌐 https://cadyhammer.com
🐦 https://twitter.com/CadyHammer
📘 https://facebook.com/cadyhammerauthor
🔗 https://instagram.com/cadyhammerauthor
🔗 https://pinterest.com/cadyahammer
🔗 https://www.tiktok.com/@cadyhammerauthor

Subscribe to my newsletter:

✉ https://dl.bookfunnel.com/bo920xlof6

Also by Cady Hammer

Don't miss these other works!

Chasing Fae

Grace Richardson is a young mortal woman whose only concerns are providing for her family, playing her violin, and spending as much time as possible with her brother, Leo. When Leo goes into service in the Fae's world as a mercenary, she expects him to return with the honor that he deserves.

When Leo suddenly dies in an unspecified accident, not a word, medal, or penny comes down from the higher-ups. Suspecting foul play, Grace disguises herself as a Fae and sneaks into the Upper Realm to get some answers. She anticipates being in way over her head, but the Fae soldier who discovers her true identity only a day in? Not so much.

Now Grace is forced to drag Aiden along as she tries to work out exactly how and why her brother died. Along the way, she has no choice but to confront her prejudices against the Fae as she attempts to sort out the difference between the honest and the dishonest. Political conspiracies, demon realm escapades, and family secrets will all lead Grace to the answers she's looking for… and some that she isn't.

Chasing War
Expect the unexpected when you take your place in Fae society.

When Grace arrives at the House of the Evening, she is instantly thrust into the world of the Fae nobility. As the heir to a throne she didn't even realize was hers, she has to navigate magical education, complex traditions, and a stepfamily she never asked for. With her new tutor, Talon, and Aiden by her side, Grace steps out into the Upper Realm as Lady of the House of the Evening only to find a war exploding under her gaze led by the House of Darkness. With minimal training and outdated laws keeping her from stepping up for the war effort, she and Aiden must quickly strategize against the invaders while searching in earnest for the remaining six prophecy members. As the war rages on and more pieces of the puzzle fall into place, Grace must make a decision about who to trust and how to lead.

Chasing The Past: A Chasing Fae Collection

From the universe of *Chasing Fae,* this short story collection highlights three characters from the House of the Evening, a lorddom of the nightlife, music, and art. Each of these characters represents an important part in Grace Richardson's past and future.

A Chance Meeting: When Amelia, Grace's future mother, meets Alexander for the first time, she is intrigued by his mysterious appearance and his disdain for the art she loves so much. She works to teach him the joy of creating and ends up learning a little bit about seizing life herself.

Taking My Place: Elise may not be as high ranking of a girl as the other daughters of the men her father works with, but she plans to find and take her place in the House of the Evening no matter who gets in her way.

Coming To Terms: Grace's half-brother, Neil, has never had to compete for anything. As the heir to the House of the Evening, he will inherit everything to make his own. But when his father brings home a bastard daughter, his world gets thrown into a tailspin.

The Ivy Labyrinth

Cady Hammer

The Ivy Labyrinth

In a world of magical instability, four high school students are chosen every year to enter the Ivy Labyrinth and attempt to break its hold on the planet. Four go in, but none come out. Now, it is Kristy, Kai, Brianna, and Ash's turn to enter the maze and solve its challenges and riddles in hopes of making it out alive. This magical realism serial will be written from four perspectives and take readers on a quest through physical and magical obstacles as the students struggle towards the center. Available on Kindle Vella and Radish!